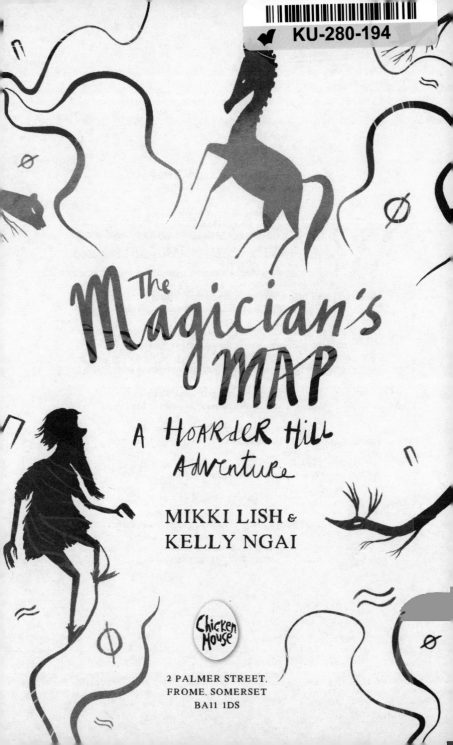

# The Magician's MAP

## A HOARDER HILL Adventure

**MIKKI LISH &**
**KELLY NGAI**

Chicken House

2 PALMER STREET,
FROME, SOMERSET
BA11 1DS

First published in Great Britain in 2021
Chicken House
2 Palmer Street
Frome, Somerset BA11 1DS
United Kingdom
www.chickenhousebooks.com

Cover and interior design by Steve Wells
Cover and interior illustration by Maxine Lee-Mackie

Typeset by Dorchester Typesetting Group Ltd
Printed and bound in Great Britain by CPI Group (UK) Ltd, Croydon CR0 4YY

The paper used in this Chicken House book is made
from wood grown in sustainable forests.

1 3 5 7 9 10 8 6 4 2

British Library Cataloguing in Publication data available.

PB 978-1-913322-56-4
eISBN 978-1-913322-88-5

## A MESSAGE FROM CHICKEN HOUSE

Welcome back to a world of fantasy and magic – my favourite bookish ingredients! I adored magic tricks when I was young, and spent hours trying to amaze my family – but the disappearing trick in the first Hoarder Hill adventure was beyond my wildest imaginings. In this startlingly clever sequel by writing master magicians Kelly and Mikki, we rejoin the resourceful cousins to explore the mysterious world of the Fantastikhana, an underground festival of magic . . . Well, what are we waiting for? Let's go!

**BARRY CUNNINGHAM**
Publisher
Chicken House

*For Brent, who agreed to a favour – K. N.*

*For Colin, who took a huge leap of faith – M. L.*

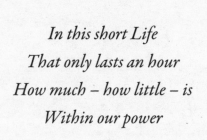

*In this short Life*
*That only lasts an hour*
*How much – how little – is*
*Within our power*

**EMILY DICKINSON**
*'In this short Life'*, Complete Poems of Emily Dickinson

# CHAPTER 1

## A LITTLE CHANGE

'Spencer! Watch out!'

Spencer van Beer risked a look behind him as he flew through the air. The stone gryphon was closing in on him, its wings flapping fast. Worse still was its outstretched talon, aiming for his ankle. He yelped. Scrunching his legs up before the gryphon could swipe him, he urged his own wings to beat faster and whooshed towards the trees.

The high-pitched whistle of his pursuer dropped away as he skirted the edge of the wood. A minute later, he swooped in amongst the tree boles, randomly flying left, right, up and down to shake the gryphon from his trail. Autumn leaves rustled in his wake.

Once he had lost count of the turns he'd taken, Spencer peeked over his shoulder. He was in the shadowy heart of the wood now. A bird darted through the air, but there was no gryphon. Perhaps he'd lost it. *Have to get back to the others*, he thought nervously. Eyes peeled, he wended his way out to the fringes of the wood, and then made the final dash for safety.

There they were, waving wildly at him. But when he was just a few metres away, the gryphon streaked out from the trees. It shot straight for him, and Spencer felt his control of the wings slip in panic. He floundered, wings beating out of time. Sensing victory, the gryphon stretched a talon towards him with an exultant screech. Spencer cartwheeled in the air and dropped clumsily to the earth, winded. He spat out a mouthful of grass as the gryphon landed on top of him and croaked, 'Tag!'

The others laughed.

'Are you OK?' his older sister Hedy asked, holding out her hand to help him to his feet. 'You looked like you tripped in mid-air.'

'Nice flying, Ginger Ninja,' called Jelly, their cousin.

'Gingers are the best kind of ninjas,' Spencer said. With an annoyed glance at the gryphon he added, 'I can't believe they won again. Hey, Max, did the gryphon cheat?'

The stone gryphon whistled indignantly at the accusation, and allowed itself to be petted by their youngest cousin, Max. 'I don't think so,' said Max. 'So Hedy still has the most points out of us.'

*Of course she does*, Spencer thought, unbuckling the enchanted metal wings that they'd borrowed from his grandfather.

'Well, I haven't had a turn in the sky yet,' said Doug the talking bear rug. He spat out the centipede he had surreptitiously licked up from the ground.

'I clearly recall *you* saying once that if you were meant to fly, you would have been born with a beak,' said Stan the stuffed stag head.

'Just because I wasn't born to do it, doesn't mean I can't,' Doug rumbled. 'By the way, you look ridiculous. What on earth has Jelly put on you?'

Jelly sat back on her heels, pleased. 'It's just a bit of lip gloss. And a bit of glitter on the antlers. And *one* stick-on jewel between the eyes. It'll come off, don't worry. Unless you want to keep it on, Stan?' She held up a small mirror for Stan to study his reflection.

'Hmm. I'm not entirely sure the effect is . . . noble,' Stan murmured doubtfully.

'But you *do* stand out,' Jelly said. 'Isn't that what you wanted? It's just the same as me and Hedy. Hedy looks amazing, see? Total stand-out now!'

Hedy tentatively touched the gem that Jelly had stuck between her own glitter-dusted eyes, at odds with her faded sweatshirt and scuffed trainers.

'There's standing out because you've got fourteen-point antlers and aren't afraid to use them, and then there's standing out like a bee sting on a weasel's backside,' Doug said. 'Now, Spencer, are we going up for a flight?'

When the sun began to sink lower in the sky, the peculiar group headed on their bikes into the village, Marberry's Rest. They'd been looking forward to this autumn holiday time together for weeks. Spencer, Hedy and their mum were visiting while their dad was on a long bike ride to raise money for a charity. As soon as it had been arranged, they'd asked for Jelly and Max to join them.

'Can you tell me again how you found Auntie Rose?' Max asked.

'Not again!' Jelly groaned. 'Max, you've heard it at least seventy-eight thousand times.'

But Hedy looked back over her shoulder at Max with a smile. She never got tired of telling him how, nearly two years ago, she and Spencer had solved the mystery of their missing Grandma Rose and rescued her from the Kaleidos.

The parts that Max really loved hearing over and over again were about how Spencer and Hedy had been helped by the many magical items that Grandpa John had hoarded and kept secret over the years. Besides Doug and Stan, there were the Woodspies who travelled through the wooden surfaces of the house, and the small stone statues known as grotesques that sat atop Grandpa John's roof to guard against intruders.

Doug was now squeezed into a milk crate on the back of Spencer's bicycle. Stan was strapped to Hedy's handlebars, and the gryphon and gargoyle sat in Jelly and Max's baskets. No one in Marberry's Rest was supposed to know that Grandpa John collected magical artefacts. Ever since the village shopkeeper,

Mrs Sutton, had once spotted Hedy flying – and had to be convinced by Grandma Rose that she must have mistaken a massive bird for a person – they were under strict instructions not to use Grandpa John's metal wings where neighbours could see them.

In the village, Doug and Stan behaved exactly as they needed to – unmoving, unblinking and silent – but the grotesques kept forgetting to stay still and had to be shushed by the children regularly.

'Wait out here,' Hedy said, standing her bike outside Sutton's General Store. The shop window was decorated for Halloween with carved jack-o'-lantern pumpkins, giant black spiders and a merry toy witch on a broomstick. 'I'll get the cake.'

An elderly couple came around the corner and the children all shuffled across the pavement to make room. Spencer had never seen them before, and he guessed they were visiting the area.

'Good afternoon,' said the man, smiling at the children and staring at Stan and Doug. 'Quite a collection you have there. Good hunting around here, then?'

He was joking of course, but hunting was a very sensitive topic for the animals. Spencer could feel

Doug rumbling low in his throat, and he saw Stan's nostrils flare.

'We're not allowed to have pets,' Spencer explained, 'so we take these around instead.'

'Oh, but I see *you're* allowed a pet,' said the woman to Max. She squinted at the gargoyle in his basket and frowned. 'Oh my, what an odd-looking cat.' By 'odd' she clearly meant ugly.

The gargoyle, instead of staying still and letting them pretend it was a statue they carted around for fun, hissed at the woman, making her gasp and clutch her husband's arm.

'I'm so sorry,' Jelly said hastily, smothering a laugh and rapping the gargoyle sharply on the head. It sank into the basket, glowering. 'We only got it from a shelter not long ago and it's not very well trained.'

Luckily, the bell of the shop door jingled and Hedy stepped out with a large cake box. The affable Mrs Sutton was right behind her.

'Hello Spencer, Angelica, Max!' she trilled. 'Taking your *pets* out for a romp, I see!' Mrs Sutton had whole-heartedly bought their cover story of not being allowed real pets, and was used to seeing them cycling around with Doug, Stan and the grotesques. She turned her attention to the newcomers. 'And welcome to our village! Where are you visiting from? Won't you come inside . . .'

The elderly couple, still taken aback by the hissing 'cat', were powerless to resist her hospitable chatter and found themselves drawn inside. Calling out their goodbyes to Mrs Sutton, the children took off.

Hoarder Hill was very different from how it had been when Spencer and Hedy had first stayed there. The gardens were filled with new shrubs and flowering plants, Grandpa John's clutter inside had been stowed away with much more order, and Grandma Rose had taken to modern appliances with great curiosity.

To the children's delight, an old milk van was parked in the driveway, which meant Mrs Pal and Soumitra had arrived for dinner. They pedalled to the back garden, where it was safest for the grotesques to return to the roof without being seen by outsiders.

'You shouldn't hiss at people,' Spencer scolded the gargoyle, making it scowl. 'If you do stuff like that, Grandpa John might not let you come out with us.'

The gargoyle's scowl deepened further as it climbed out of the basket. Its only acknowledgement of

Spencer was a stone pellet that it sulkily ejected from its bottom. Apologizing was not in the grotesques' natures.

'Did Fluffy do another one?' Max clapped. He liked to collect the stone pellets, and his insistence on calling the grotesques by babyish names often inspired even more petulant droppings.

The gryphon let loose stone pellets of its own (in support of the gargoyle rather than out of kindness to Max), then the pair flapped up to the top of the house, muttering to themselves.

'The mighty challengers return!' called Grandpa John as he walked up from the bottom of the garden. By his side were Mrs Pal, the owner of a magic shop called the Palisade, and a young man – her grandson, Soumitra. The children ran to hug them.

'Who won?' asked Soumitra.

'The grotesques did, *again*. Only Hedy can ever beat them at flying,' Spencer groaned.

'Just keep trying and you'll catch up,' Soumitra grinned. 'Who's going to give me the race highlights? Stan?'

Stan, carried by Jelly, lit up. 'Why, I'd be delighted, and can only hope that my reflections adequately chronicle the heroism of the tourney!'

'That might be the first time anyone's ever described the grotesques as heroic,' Grandpa John mused.

As Hedy, Jelly and Max went ahead to the house with Soumitra, Grandpa John held Spencer back for a moment.

'What's wrong?' Spencer asked.

'I'm sorry, Spencer,' said Mrs Pal, 'but we'll have to postpone your visit to the Palisade. I have an event to go to. We'll make another time, I promise.'

Spencer tried to disguise his disappointment. He'd had an idea of modifying his Polaroid camera in a special – well, slightly magical – way, and he could think of no one better with whom to figure it out than Mrs Pal. 'Where are you going?'

'It's called the Fantastikhana,' said Mrs Pal.

A thrill rippled through Spencer, making the hairs on the back of his neck stand up. 'Can I go with you?'

'You don't even know what it is,' Grandpa John snorted.

'But it *sounds* good. What is it?'

'It's a gathering of fusty old people like me,' said Grandpa John.

Mrs Pal, however, tutted and said, 'There's a youth competition for magic, and workshops where children can get together and tinker. A bit like those arts-and-crafts workshops in the school holidays.'

Spencer's mind was awhirl. 'But with *magic*?'

'Low-level magic, I imagine, not the exciting stuff you're after,' said Grandpa John.

'But it sounds perfect!' Spencer cried. 'Please can we go?'

Grandpa John turned to Mrs Pal sourly. 'Did you plan this?'

'It seems like the perfect opportunity, Mr Sang,' she said innocently.

Spencer hopped around his grandfather. 'Please? I really want to learn how to make stuff like Mrs Pal. Maybe I can run the Palisade when I grow up.' He suddenly broke off, wondering if he'd overstepped the mark. 'I mean, if Soumitra doesn't want to.'

'Good grief!' Grandpa John exclaimed. 'I thought this was an idea for a hobby, not your life's ambition.'

*Oops*, thought Spencer, and pulled a face to make it seem like a joke. How could he convince Grandpa John to go to this Fantastikhana and take them with him?

'Don't you want to talk with other magicians?' he asked.

Grandpa John shook his head firmly. 'Not if I can help it.'

## CHAPTER 2

### THE INVITATION

'Happy birthday to you!'

Mrs Pal took a deep breath to blow out the candles, but a gust of wind beat her to it, making them all laugh. It was a fine autumn evening, so they were eating on the back patio under cheery strings of lights, with Doug hanging over a chair and Stan wedged between Mum and Soumitra. The children were perched on the stone bench upon which Grandpa John's former cook, Mrs Vilums, and her sisters had once sat as statues.

'Uncle John, use some magic to light the candles

again!' Max urged.

'Matches are just fine, Max,' Grandpa John said. Although he still collected new artefacts, Grandpa John remained adamant about avoiding the practice of magic.

'Can't you just bend the rules once in a while?' Hedy asked. 'Like a magical windbreak? That wouldn't do anyone any harm.'

'If I knew how,' Spencer said, 'I'd make birthday candles that didn't blow out unless the person doing the blowing had made a wish.'

Mrs Pal tapped her chin, intrigued. 'The difficulty there would be finding and channelling the power to bestow wishes.'

'What *could* do that?' asked Jelly.

'Oh, please,' Grandpa John said, 'let's not encourage Spencer to experiment with djinns or magical fish or any of that nonsense. Folklore tells us it's disaster.'

'How is the shop, Rani?' Grandma Rose asked.

'There's been a lull in business for a few weeks,' said Mrs Pal. 'But that's not so surprising, because a lot of trade will be happening this weekend.'

'Someone tried to break in a week ago,' said Soumitra darkly.

'That's awful,' Hedy exclaimed. 'What happened?'

'My security system scared them off before they could get in,' Mrs Pal assured her. 'Whoever it was had a big fall off the roof out the back, but they managed to run away.'

'Maybe it's time to move the shop out of that area,' suggested Grandpa John.

Mrs Pal waved away his concern. 'There are reasons I'm in that spot.'

'A lot of trade this weekend, did you say?' said Stan. 'Do you mean the Fantastikhana is taking place?'

Hedy's ears pricked up. 'What's that?'

Grandpa John shot Stan an aggrieved look. 'As I told Spencer, it's a get-together of grumpy old folk like me whose best years of magic are behind them.'

'But you said there are workshops where we could do magic arts and crafts,' Spencer reminded him.

'And that's not all,' said Stan. 'I was once at a Fantastikhana, being traded from one owner to another. There's bartering, there are a great many stalls, and there's a competition for children about Hedy's size or bigger. Youngsters have to complete feats of magic to win.'

All four children began talking over one another,

clamouring to go to this event with the odd-sounding name. At last Grandpa John held up his hand. 'It's not the sort of place I want to take you. There are too many unpredictable things at a Fantastikhana.' In his mind, 'unpredictable' equalled 'dangerous'.

'But won't they keep a lid on the dangerous stuff?' Jelly asked.

Grandpa John grunted. 'You'd be surprised how incompetent they can be.'

'Mrs Pal thinks it's all right!' said Spencer.

'And if it's OK for other kids to go and *compete*, it must be OK for us to go and *watch*,' Hedy said. 'Please, can't we do something really fun as a family for once?'

'Your grandmother doesn't want to go,' said Grandpa John sharply, 'so put it out of your mind.'

The children fell silent.

Grandma Rose didn't bother to hide the exasperated glance she threw in Grandpa John's direction. 'I'm going to put the kettle on.' She held her hand out to Hedy. 'Keep me company?'

As they walked to the kitchen, Hedy kept hold of her grandmother's hand, which she'd never do with her parents now that she was thirteen years old. But she sensed that her grandmother found comfort in it and here, at Hoarder Hill, Hedy didn't find it embarrassing.

In fact, a lot of things weren't embarrassing here but very much *were* in the outside world. Hedy had learnt that the hard way; the rules had changed when she hadn't been paying attention. Telling your best friend that you knew a talking bear rug and stag head, and had met a ghost pianist – *and* saved your grandmother from a magic disappearing box – was OK in primary school. In secondary school it made you a weirdo, and all of a sudden you had to make new friends and keep the most interesting thing in your life secret, and make yourself very, very ordinary.

Grandma Rose plucked a square of thick black card from the fridge. 'He was invited to the Fantastikhana, you know,' she said. 'This is his invitation. But he turned it down. He still doesn't trust that group of people – but the main reason he didn't go is that he didn't want to leave me on my own.'

'But you wouldn't be on your own,' Hedy said brightly. 'Not if we all went together.'

Grandma Rose grimaced. 'I don't really want to be answering questions the whole time I'm there. They know that I was found after thirty years being missing.

They'll want to know where I was.'

'So you're kind of famous?' Hedy asked. 'That's cool.'

'I don't want to be gawked at, Hedy,' Grandma Rose said gently. 'And I'm not ready to talk about the inside of the Kaleidos.'

Hedy stared at the Fantastikhana invitation. Embossed with silvery print, it was from some group called the Sleight, and was made out to the Amazing John Sang. As Hedy traced her finger over the elaborate F insignia at the bottom, she heard a faint sound, like a carnival: many voices talking indistinctly, music playing, bells ringing, far-off applause.

Lost in thought, Hedy didn't notice Grandpa John and Mrs Pal passing through the kitchen until her grandpa cupped her cheek. 'I'm sorry I snapped,' he said.

'It's OK.'

Hedy helped Grandma Rose take the tea things out to the patio and everyone tucked into slices of cake. Then, on a hunch, she volunteered to fetch Grandpa John and Mrs Pal.

The study door was closed, as expected. After months of commonplace conversations about bands and crushes and homework and football training,

Hedy realized she felt starved in a very particular way: starved of hearing about magic, of feeling she was part of something special and significant. She knew it was wrong to eavesdrop, but she put her ear to the door anyway. Their words were muffled, though.

*I should just knock*, Hedy thought. She raised her hand, but before she could knock, a bump appeared in the wood, gently nuzzling her cheek. It was the littlest Woodspy.

'Hello,' she whispered. She didn't even have to ask. The Woodspy knew what she wanted in her heart right at that moment, and obligingly pulled a tiny bit of the door's edge inwards, enough to make a gap through which Hedy could hear the conversation.

'I'm lucky Rosie made me get organized and inventory my things,' Grandpa John was saying. 'I'd barely thought of this mirror in years.'

Hedy put her eye to the gap in the door. They were talking about a small round piece of metal, about the size of a saucer. One side had an elaborate design etched into the surface, and the other side was plain and mirrored.

'Well, Brock Rabble wants to meet you and me this weekend.'

'Brock Rabble!' exclaimed Grandpa John.

Mrs Pal nodded. 'He must have somehow heard you had the mirror. He claims he has information about it.'

Grandpa John looked torn. 'I already turned down the invitation from the Sleight, and I didn't exactly mince my words on my opinion of them. If I show up now, they'll wonder why I changed my mind.'

'Bring the children,' Mrs Pal suggested. 'It's a credible excuse – you brought them there to see the competition.'

'I don't want to leave Rose here on her own.'

'What if someone stayed here with her?'

Hedy whispered her thanks to the Woodspy and scuttled back outside, thinking fast. The only way Grandpa John would feel comfortable leaving their grandmother was if Grandma Rose suggested it herself and had Hedy's mum, Olivia, for company. And with Dad on the charity bike ride, it was the perfect arrangement for Mum too. Hedy slipped in between Grandma Rose and Mum and whispered to them, so that by the time Grandpa John returned to the table, everything had been worked out.

'It's unfair to hold you back, John,' said Grandma

Rose. 'Why don't Olivia and I have a girls' weekend here, while you take the kids to the Fantastikhana?'

In the morning, all four children woke up very early, trying – and failing – to keep their excited chatter to whispers. The Fantastikhana ran for three days, so they were going to be away for two nights with Grandpa John.

They all raced through breakfast and the washing-up, and then – as they did every morning at Hoarder Hill – stopped by Doug and Stan's room to give Doug his daily 'massage', which was in fact a gentle vacuuming of his fur.

Stan looked at Doug with a critical eye. 'The most decadent emperor of Rome never enjoyed such treatment.'

'I'll wager the most decadent emperor of Rome was never turned into a rug,' Doug said. 'Nor shaved from neck to rump. *Nor* had a tail lopped off. I think I'm allowed a bit of pampering now and then.'

'Children,' said Stan peevishly, 'the Fantastikhana will have stalls selling all different kinds of things. If you find something that will make fur grow, would you bring some home for that shaved stripe down

Doug's back? The martyr won't suffer in noble silence, and I'd rather not have to hear him suffering any longer.'

Jelly's eyes sparkled with possibility. 'Shopping list! Why didn't I think of that?'

'If only we could go with you as well,' Stan sighed. 'Wouldn't that be grand? It would be so enjoyable to see everything properly, without the stress of being traded.'

'I wish you could come too,' said Hedy, patting Stan's head. 'Have any of you guys heard of the Sleight?'

'You mean like "sleight of hand"?' Max asked. 'That's card tricks and those close-up magic tricks.'

Hedy shrugged. 'Grandpa John's invitation to the Fantastikhana was from the Sleight, so it sounds like a group of people.'

'I believe the Sleight are a group of, well, magicians,' said Stan. 'Senior magicians, is my understanding.'

That got Spencer's attention. 'Do you mean stage magicians or real magicians?'

'Real ones,' Stan said.

'And what do the Sleight do?' asked Hedy.

'That I do not know. Doug, do you know anything about them?'

Doug flicked an ear. 'I only heard them mentioned once, at a previous Master's house. And from that, I gather the Sleight are a group of magicians who get together and make each other irritable.'

## CHAPTER 3

## THE SECOND COUSIN (ONCE REMOVED)

'Grandpa John, how are we going to fit Mrs Pal in the car?' Spencer asked as the car hummed towards Mrs Pal's shop.

'We don't have to drive to the Fantastikhana,' Grandpa John replied.

'Are we catching the bus or something?'

'Or something.'

Mrs Pal was waiting outside with a bag, her walking stick and Soumitra when Grandpa John parked at the back of the Palisade. The children tumbled out of the car excitedly.

'Are you coming too?' Spencer asked Soumitra.

'Sorry, buddy,' Soumitra said, 'I've got to look after the shop while you all go and have fun.'

'A little responsibility is good for you,' Mrs Pal said, patting Soumitra's hand.

'Yeah, but a festival of magic would be even better!'

'Stake your claim on the shop now, Soumitra,' Grandpa John advised. 'If you don't, Spencer will sneak in and take over the Palisade while you're not looking. Mrs Pal, we're not late, are we?'

'No,' Mrs Pal said. 'But I'm not very fast, so we'd better go to the meeting point now, if we want to get there for nine-thirty.'

The meeting point was a few streets away: a flight of steps that ran between two old buildings, and led upwards to the parallel street at the top of the hill. Up the centre of the stairs was a handrail punctuated every few metres with ornamental lion heads. The steps themselves were smooth and worn down in the middle by the many feet that had trudged, marched or skipped up and down them over the years.

'Are we supposed to wait here or at the top?' Hedy asked.

'Right here,' Mrs Pal said, standing at the base of the handrail.

Grandpa John studied the stairs. 'I didn't realize you had an entry point so close to the shop.'

Mrs Pal smiled. 'That's why I opened the shop here.'

Spencer and Max raced each other up the stairs to slide down the handrail. When Spencer, sliding head first, reached the bottom, he found the first lion's head at the very end of the handrail looking him up and down.

'Argh!' he yelped, falling to the ground in shock.

Mrs Pal didn't seem startled at all. She chuckled and leant closer to the squinting lion's head. 'Rani Pal.' She nodded at Grandpa John to move in closer.

Glancing around to make sure no strangers were watching, he said, 'John Sang.'

The lion's head seemed startled at the mention of Grandpa John's name. But it nodded respectfully and let out a short roar – not very loud, but it was echoed by all the other lion heads up the handrail. Spencer squeezed Max's hand in excitement.

One by one, the stairs changed. They began to sink into the earth, reversing their rise, so that instead of a staircase leading upwards to another street, it became a staircase dropping down towards a very dark tunnel.

Out of the darkness bobbed a lantern. Someone was trotting up the steps.

It was a middle-aged man with short dark hair, and he seemed out of breath. On each of his shoulders perched a white parrot with a bright-yellow crest.

'I'm late,' one parrot screeched, only to be hushed by the man with some embarrassment. Evidently, he had been muttering that to himself on the way there. He wiped his hand on his trouser leg and held it out to Mrs Pal. 'Hello, Mrs Pal. I'm Ewan Tsang. We spoke on the phone.' He had a thick Scottish accent.

Mrs Pal shook Ewan's hand. 'Thank you for coming to collect us. This is John Sang.'

'I know,' Ewan said, and he shook Grandpa John's hand reverently. 'It's an honour. I didn't expect to ever meet you, Mr Sang.'

'It was a bit last-minute,' Grandpa John admitted. 'Call me John, please.'

Ewan smiled shyly. Then he looked around at the children and Soumitra with a worried expression. 'Ah. There are more of you than I was instructed to collect.'

'These are my grandchildren, and my brother's

grandchildren,' Grandpa John said. 'Everybody ganged up on me to bring them along.'

Looking trapped, Ewan said, 'The problem is, I don't think they'll be on the list to get in.'

Spencer's heart sank. They were so close to going – they couldn't let themselves be turned away now! He grabbed Grandpa John's hand pleadingly.

Grandpa John weighed something up. 'Surely you could do something for your cousins?' he said to Ewan.

'Cousins!' Spencer exclaimed.

'If I've got this correct, Ewan is your second cousin once removed,' said Grandpa John.

'My great-grandfather is John's grandfather,' Ewan added with a note of pride.

The children stared at the two men. The pieces were falling into place now: Grandpa John's and Uncle Peter's surname, 'Sang', was an anglicized form of 'Tsang'. Their great-great-grandfather, Tsang Li Ming, had been a magician; Grandpa John had followed in his footsteps.

'What do you think, Ewan?' Grandpa John prodded.

Ewan shifted anxiously from foot to foot. 'I've got a

little wagon down there for your bags, but it won't fit seven people's.'

'We'll carry our own backpacks,' Spencer promised.

'And we'll be super well-behaved,' Jelly added. 'Low profile. Totally under the radar.'

'Mr Sang – I mean, John,' Ewan caught himself, 'don't forget that once you're below in the Fantastikhana, there's no contact with the overground for those three days. Phones don't work down there.'

'Our mum knows,' Spencer assured him. It was true, although Mum had asked Grandpa John and Hedy to send a message if they ever got a bar of reception on their phones.

One of the parrots squawked, 'Second cousin once removed!'

'But cousins,' replied the other.

Ewan's resistance crumbled. 'All right, come along and I'll do what fast-talking I can.' He turned to Soumitra. 'And are you a cousin too?'

Soumitra laughed. 'No, I'm the poor sucker staying behind to look after the shop.'

'Maybe at the next Fantastikhana, then.' Ewan eyed Mrs Pal's walking stick. 'Mrs Pal, will you be all right with a ten- or fifteen-minute walk?'

She nodded. 'I might be slow, but it's not a problem.'

'Well, we'd best be off.'

Soumitra gave Mrs Pal a hug and, with a wistful wave, backed away from the top step as everyone else made their way down into the tunnel. The lions on the handrail roared again and, step by step, the reversed stone staircase rose up, resuming its normal slope. Soumitra and the street above were lost from view. No one up there would have had a clue that the stairs were remarkable in any way.

There was a small wagon at the bottom of the staircase, in which Ewan carefully stowed Mrs Pal's and Grandpa John's bags. Then he held up his lantern to light the way for their walk.

The tunnel was large enough that they could walk three abreast without touching the walls of dark earth. At first everyone was dumbstruck by the surroundings, and the only sounds were the trundling wheels of the wagon and their footsteps, in particular the *klok klok* noise of Jelly's clogs. But soon enough, Ewan began to chatter.

The parrots, he told them, were sulphur-crested cockatoos named Chit and Chat. 'They're part of my inheritance,' he said a little sourly. 'They make a racket if I don't take them around enough. They go virtually everywhere with me except the bedroom and the bathroom.'

'A stinker!' said one bird, apparently triggered by the mention of 'bathroom'.

'Light a match!' answered the other. The children burst into giggles.

'The only thing they're good for is this.' To the birds, Ewan said, 'Light up.'

'Light up, *please*,' reminded a cockatoo.

Ewan sighed. 'Light up, please.'

The cockatoos' crests began to glow with a cool yellow light. One of the birds lifted a wing and more light radiated from its underwing, illuminating the tunnel far better than the lantern.

By now, the tunnel wall had changed from packed dirt to rough-hewn pale limestone. It smelt damp down here, and the air was warmer than at the steps.

'How far do we have to go?' Grandpa John asked.

'Only a wee bit longer,' Ewan said, 'maybe five minutes.'

Max began to dart in and out of the light thrown by the cockatoos. 'Does the Fantastikhana have rides?'

'Erm. No, I'm afraid not,' Ewan said. 'But I think you'll like the tournament. Youngsters have to complete feats of magic to win.'

'Oh!' Max skipped to Ewan's side. 'Can I enter? Can I compete?'

'Sorry, you're a bit young.'

'How old do you have to be?'

'Between thirteen and eighteen years old.'

Over Max's groan, Jelly said, 'So me and Hedy can enter?'

'No one is entering the tournament,' Grandpa John said.

'Why not?'

'You wouldn't enter a music competition without having learnt to play an instrument.'

A few minutes later, their tunnel joined a large paved-brick passageway with an arched ceiling. Ewan seemed relieved. 'There, that didn't take too long, did it?'

A labyrinth of smaller, empty chambers opened off the passageway. As Spencer checked out one of the less dim and spooky ones, Jelly – who seemed more clumsy than usual in these tunnels – tripped into his side.

'Why do you wear those things?' Spencer asked, looking at her clogs. 'You keep tripping in them.'

'They used to be my mum's and they're cool,' Jelly muttered. 'I didn't know we'd be walking this much.'

'Mrs Pal,' Spencer said, 'did you know these tunnels were in Stradmoor?'

'Oh, we're not in Stradmoor any more,' Ewan said over his shoulder. 'We're in Edinburgh now. We've linked to the South Bridge vaults, but the Fantastikhana is being held on the other side of them.'

'Edinburgh?' exclaimed Hedy. 'As in Scotland?'

'Aye.' Ewan smiled at the bewilderment on the children's faces.

'But Scotland is a whole day's drive away!'

Ewan's smile grew even wider. 'It is. That's why it was quicker for you not to travel by car. These tunnels are special.'

Spencer stared at the walls of the vault in wonder. Besides being underground, the walk had felt quite ordinary. He'd had no sense that they had somehow skipped hundreds of kilometres. 'Grandpa John, have you ever come through a tunnel like this?'

'Not in a very long time, Spencer,' he said. 'And I've never been here.'

'Are there ghosts down here?' Max asked, shrinking into Jelly's side.

Ewan gave Max a reassuring shake of the head. 'There may be ghosts and poltergeists floating around the vaults, but those troublemakers aren't getting into the Fantastikhana. We've put up protective wards to keep them out. Right, Mr Boo?'

He had stopped in front of an immense bricked-in archway. Before it was a black bollard, the top of which was shaped like a horse's head with a white star on its brow. The horse head put back its ears and snorted. 'Why must you insist on calling me that?'

'Bucephalus!' squawked Chit.

'Most famous horse in history!' added Chat.

'You used to like me calling you Mr Boo,' protested Ewan.

Bucephalus whickered. 'You're not eight any more, Ewan. You're a grown man and a member of the Sleight. Act like it. You're rather late.'

Mrs Pal lifted up her walking stick. 'That's my fault. I don't walk terribly fast.'

'My apologies, madam,' the horse head said, more politely. 'Could you all line up, please.' His tone made Spencer feel like snapping to attention with his chin up and shoulders thrown back. 'Who do we have?'

'Rani Pal,' Mrs Pal said.

'A maker. Welcome. Next?'

Spencer, Hedy, Jelly and Max all gave their names. Bucephalus was silent for a few moments. 'Not on the list.'

'You're right,' Ewan said, 'but as soon as we get inside, I'll find Candice and I'm *absolutely* sure that she'll say they can attend.'

'If they're not on the list, they can't go in.'

'Mr—' Ewan caught himself. 'Bucephalus, we can't leave them out here in the Slip. I know Candice will be OK with it, so we may as well go in now, together.'

'Why are you so sure Candice will agree?'

Ewan waved at Grandpa John. 'This is my cousin, John Sang!'

After a long look at Grandpa John, the horse head said, 'I need to hear *him* say his name to check whether he's on the list or not.'

Grandpa John stepped forward. 'I'm John Sang.'

Ewan couldn't help himself. 'The Amazing John Sang!'

'Indeed?' Bucephalus sounded a little impressed. 'Magician. Welcome.'

'So, can we go in too?' Spencer asked.

'There's no contact with the standard overground once you're inside,' said Bucephalus. 'Not until the Fantastikhana is finished. We can't have the wrong people knowing what goes on here. Do you understand?'

*Who are the wrong people?* Spencer wondered.

But Grandpa John simply said, 'We understand.'

'Very well,' the horse sighed. 'Ewan, make sure you get Candice's approval. I don't want to have to send in someone to throw them out.' He directed them to stand on the flagstones in front of the archway, then neighed, 'Arms, legs and tails in, everyone!'

There was a grinding noise of stone on stone as the archway and the flagstones began to rotate in the wall and the floor of the tunnel. It was a huge secret revolving door.

A clamour burst through from the other side of the wall, the noise of hundreds of people chattering over live music. When the archway and flagstones stopped rotating, they stepped out into a crowd of people moving around a huge underground cavern. Here was the Fantastikhana.

## CHAPTER 4

## CHAMBER AND PARLOUR

'Lights out,' Ewan told the birds as a few people looked them over curiously. Both cockatoos settled their wings and allowed their yellow glow to fade.

The cavern looked like a cross between an arena and a country fair. Forming a ring around the outside were many colourful, busy stalls, selling food, clothes, flags and a lot of other things Hedy couldn't take in all at once. Flourishing trees and neat grassy lawns were strewn throughout the cavern, just right for picnicking. Towards the centre of the cavern was a large open stage. Stagehands bustled about, carrying what looked like competition paraphernalia: poles, barricades, flags and large spheres.

'Is the competition starting now?' she asked Ewan.

He shook his head. 'There'll be the opening ceremony in a little while, and the competition will start shortly after that. Let's go and find Candice and get your approval sorted out. I don't fancy being tracked by Bucephalus's minions.'

Ewan led them through the crowded cavern into a corridor that could have belonged to any grand old building. He stopped at a door painted a beautiful teal colour. 'This is the Peacock Chamber.' After a moment's wait, the door opened of its own accord.

Hedy had visited a few castles with her family, but this room was far more splendid than any castle room she had ever seen. Floating in the air was a large chandelier, and the walls were traced all over with blues and greens and golds that shifted gently like feathers in a breeze. Along one wall was a sideboard set with heaped platters of fruit and pastries. In the centre of the room was a large table surrounded by chairs that each had a different bird carved into the back panel. The grandest chair, at the head of the table, was carved with a peacock.

An elegant grey-haired woman turned at their interruption. 'Is this important, Ewan?' Then she pursed her lips in recognition. 'Ah. I won't be long.'

She turned back to the two people she had been speaking with. There was a girl around Hedy's age, with tidy braids and determined blue eyes that were more intimidating than her heavy-soled black boots. Hedy felt judged by those eyes, and she couldn't help raking her fingers through her own messy hair. Next to the girl was a man whose arm was in a plaster cast and sling. He must have been the girl's father, for he had the same blue eyes, although he had a goofy smile and a less forbidding look than the girl.

'Well, I'm impressed that you detected and trapped a poltergeist, Beatrice,' the woman said. She inspected something small in her hand that looked like a walnut shell.

'She made a tough nut even tougher to crack!' said the father proudly.

'She's obviously quite gifted. Beatrice, I look forward to seeing what you can do here at the Fantastikhana.'

The girl pointed to the walnut. 'Where will you put it, Ms Harding? A strongbox or something?'

'We'll keep it secure until we decide where it can safely be expelled,' the woman assured her, slipping it into her pocket. 'Now, I dare say you'd like to go and get ready for the opening ceremony?'

The pair of them left, the father murmuring a cheery hello to them all, although his smile faltered when he passed Mrs Pal. He ushered his daughter out of the room hurriedly.

'Hello, Candice,' said Ewan. 'I met Mrs Rani Pal and Mr John Sang as arranged – and, uh, Mr Sang brought his grandchildren and his brother's grandchildren along.'

Candice Harding offered her hand – adorned with a dazzling sapphire ring that prompted a loud sigh from Jelly – to Mrs Pal.

'Rani,' said Candice, 'I'm very glad you accepted our invitation.' Then she turned to Grandpa John. 'I'm extremely surprised to see you here, John. You made your thoughts about the Sleight pretty clear.'

Grandpa John shook her offered hand guardedly. 'The children got wind of what was on this weekend and they were keen to see what it was like.'

Hedy suddenly found herself the subject of Candice's gaze. It was hard not to squirm, and she did her best to smile politely. She was sure that whenever people sat around the table, Candice was the one who sat in the peacock chair.

The woman studied each of the children, and then her eyes flickered between Hedy and Jelly. 'And which is the girl who found and saved Rose?'

Hedy stiffened. 'M-me.'

'Remarkable,' said Candice warmly. 'I'm sure I haven't even heard the full story of what you did. It must be fascinating. John, you really should have brought Rose with you.' At the prickle of Candice's probing expression, Hedy understood exactly why Grandma Rose hadn't wanted to come. 'What's your name?'

'Hedy.'

'And how far along in your training are you, Hedy?'

Hedy gaped blankly at Candice, feeling stupid. Clearing his throat, Grandpa John said, 'They're not receiving any training.'

Candice's perfectly groomed eyebrows shot up. 'Why? Doesn't she have a gift?'

'No,' Grandpa John said, 'no gifts besides a touch of disobedience. But she has heart.'

'Didn't you bring them here to compete in the Fantastikhana?' Candice asked.

*Heart doesn't seem to impress Candice much*, Hedy thought, trying not to feel belittled.

Grandpa John shook his head. 'They're not like those children. They just want to watch some of the competition.'

'And I want to do a workshop!' Spencer piped up.

That seemed to amuse Candice. 'Do we have a young maker in this one?'

'He's only dabbling,' Grandpa John said.

'Quite possibly,' Mrs Pal declared at the exact same moment.

Candice glided to the side table and picked out a pastry. 'Excuse me for eating. I haven't had breakfast yet – been run off my feet, what with the opening ceremony in a short while. All right, I'll have the children added to the attendee list. John, I hope you'll reconsider being a mentor while you're here.'

Grandpa John shrugged. 'If I had any useful knowledge to impart, I would. But I don't. Sorry.'

'Ms Harding,' Mrs Pal said, 'do you know where we might find Brock Rabble?'

Candice nodded. 'Probably at Pick Pocket Parlour, telling stories. Why do you need Rabble?' She took a bite of her pastry, but Hedy could tell that her indifferent manner hid a real curiosity.

'Simply to catch up,' Mrs Pal said.

Candice glanced at Grandpa John to see if he'd give away anything more, but he was silent. Finally, she said, 'Well, enjoy your time here.'

'Can we look around now?' Spencer asked Grandpa John as they all left the Peacock Chamber.

'Look around at what?' Grandpa John said. 'The competition hasn't started yet.'

'Can't we go and find a workshop?'

'Or look at the stalls,' Jelly added. 'I bet they're selling stuff you can't get above ground.'

Max hopped up and down. 'I want something to eat.'

'You only just nicked a pasty in the Peacock Chamber!' Jelly scolded.

'No, I didn't!'

'I *saw* you!'

Ignoring the squabble, Grandpa John and Mrs Pal quietly conferred, then asked Ewan to show them to Pick Pocket Parlour. He led them to a grand tunnel intersection. 'Pick Pocket Parlour is down that way,' he said, pointing down one passageway. 'The main cavern is signposted, so you won't have to look too hard to get back to it.'

'Why's it called Pick Pocket Parlour?' Hedy asked.

'Well, its actual name is just the Parlour,' Ewan said. 'But everybody calls it Pick Pocket Parlour because a lot of people get pickpocketed there. I don't know why people insist on doing business at the Parlour, but they do.'

Ewan, Chit and Chat bade them farewell with a promise to catch up with them later on, to take them to their hotel.

'I don't want to go to a parlour,' Max complained as they walked along. 'It sounds boring.'

'We could've left you at home, you know,' Jelly said. 'This is the first time Uncle John's taken us anywhere. If you keep on moaning—'

'I'm *not* moaning!'

'Well, if you keep whingeing, he won't – *oof!*' At that moment, Jelly tripped yet again. 'I wish I'd never borrowed these stupid clogs!'

'Ha!' Max crowed. 'That's what happens when you wear canoes on your feet.'

Hedy couldn't help smiling at 'canoes', despite the glare it earned from Jelly. 'They are a bit weird-looking.'

'That's why they're cool,' Jelly huffed. 'They're *vintage*. You wouldn't understand.'

Smarting, Hedy lost her smile. She knew she wasn't as quirky and cool as her cousin and, when it came to fashion, she often felt like the age difference between them was greater than a year.

Grandpa John and Mrs Pal had drawn to a stop at a massive wooden door with a sign that read *The Parlour*. 'Are you ready to stop bickering or do I have to leave you out here in the passageway?' he said warningly.

They all muttered they'd get along.

'All right. Keep close, please, and keep quiet.'

The Parlour had an air of secrecy. Small groups of men and women conferred in alcoves, or in velvet booths, or at the long counter where drinks were served. The walls were covered to their last inch with paintings of all styles and subjects. As Hedy's eyes adjusted to the dim light, she picked out some disturbingly familiar paintings amongst the collection: Theries, those half-human, half-animal creatures which, as she had discovered two years ago at Hoarder Hill, could reach out of the paintings to steal things.

'Spence,' Hedy whispered, gripping her brother's arm, 'I bet the Therie paintings are why this place is called Pick Pocket Parlour.'

A burst of laughter drifted from the far end of the room. 'That will be Rabble,' Mrs Pal said to Grandpa John.

As they picked their way between tables, Hedy could feel eyes flicker over them curiously. She was mostly sure the eyes belonged to the people around them, rather than the paintings.

Brock Rabble, the man they had been looking for, was sitting in a large velvet booth, surrounded by an attentive group of young men and women. From the looks of it, they had been listening to his stories for quite some time. He waved a pair of bright-purple glasses around as he recounted his tale, but upon seeing Grandpa John and Mrs Pal approaching, Rabble stopped mid-sentence and popped the glasses on to his nose.

'Blow me down, what are John Sang and Rani Pal doing underground?' he cried.

'Hello, Rabble,' Grandpa John said. 'Been a long time.'

Rabble began to shoo his listeners from his booth. 'I'll finish the story later, come back in an hour!' As they shuffled away, Hedy overheard the young men and women murmuring things like, 'he was a magician *ages* ago,' and 'a maker, she runs the Palisade.' A waiter cleared away the many glasses from the tabletop and Rabble hoisted himself to his feet to greet them. He was quite short, and had an enormous forehead topped by wisps of hair like a baby's. His purple glasses complemented his rumpled suit of mauve and violet.

'What brings you two sly devils here?' Rabble asked.

Both Grandpa John and Mrs Pal frowned at him, baffled.

'*You* invited us here,' said Mrs Pal.

Scratching his head, Rabble murmured, 'I did?'

Mrs Pal showed him a letter from her handbag.

'I don't remember writing this,' the old man said. 'But I have so many memories sitting in this old noggin that sometimes one or two fall out. Map and mirror, eh? Let's talk.'

Mrs Pal looked pointedly around the Parlour. 'Is there somewhere we can speak privately?'

'There most certainly is.' Rabble pulled a piece of chalk from his pocket and made a few scratchy marks on the wall behind him and on two spots of the velvet booth. ('I'll clean it off,' he told the reproving waiter, 'or a tenner for you if you clean it off for me.') Then he held out the chalk to Hedy. 'Here, lass. Draw a half-circle on the floor for me, from that end of the booth to the other. You're marking off the territory.'

As Hedy bent down to do as he instructed, she spotted old remnants of chalk marks that hadn't been entirely rubbed away. *Rabble must do this quite a bit*, she thought.

Once Hedy had finished, Rabble reached under the table and then produced what looked like a small conch shell of pale-green jade. He set it on the table surface, and spun it like a spinning top. As it twirled, the steady chatter of the Parlour grew softer and softer until, when the shell at last came to rest, there was no sound at all but their booth. The rest of Pick Pocket Parlour looked darkened, as though it were behind a heavily tinted window.

'There we are, private as a confessional,' Rabble said. 'Now, what've you got?'

## CHAPTER 5

## A MAP MOORED

Mrs Pal placed her arm on the table and drew up her sleeve. A black line snaked around her wrist. Spencer thought she was showing Rabble one of her tattoos, but it couldn't be an ordinary tattoo because the line in her skin was rippling.

'What is *that*?' Jelly asked, horrified. 'Please tell me it's not a worm in your skin.'

'Goodness, Jelly, it's not a worm,' Mrs Pal chuckled.

'What *is* it, then? Why is it moving?'

'It can help find things,' Mrs Pal said simply.

Rabble was fascinated. 'Where did you get it?'

'I made it.'

The old man goggled at her. 'I've not heard of anyone making a new unmoored map in my time. I've seen inherited ones, passed down through the family, but not a wee one like this. I'm impressed.'

Mrs Pal shrugged modestly. 'I experiment, and sometimes it works.'

All the children bent over Mrs Pal's wrist to get a better look. 'What's an unmoored map?' Hedy asked.

'It's like a map seedling,' Rabble said. 'It can be repurposed with the right magic. You can have it guide you to one thing, then give it new moorings and it will guide you to another. They were used a lot more in the old days.'

Spencer's eyes lit up. 'So it could show me the way to *anything*? Like, treasure chests that haven't been discovered yet?'

'Only if someone created a set of instructions to find that treasure chest, with a starting point, an end point and bearings in between. Those instructions are the moorings, you see. They give the map direction and purpose. It's fancy magic to create moorings. And they're sometimes hidden, too, for extra secrecy. The problem with this wee map is that it has no moorings.'

Rabble smirked at Mrs Pal. 'You need me to find moorings for you to buy, don't you? So that the map has something to find.'

Mrs Pal shook her head. 'Your turn, Mr Sang.'

Grandpa John reached into his inside jacket pocket and pulled out a small cloth bag. In it was a round mirror, with an ornate pattern on its back.

Rabble slapped his hand on the tabletop, startling everybody. 'A Chinese magic mirror! Where did you get it?'

'It's been handed down through my family,' Grandpa John said. 'I believe my grandfather made it.'

'Tsang Li Ming?' Rabble asked.

Grandpa John nodded. 'And from what I've been told, it has instructions for an unmoored map in it.' He paused, looking sheepish. 'But we don't know how it works.'

'That I can show you,' said Rabble with a Cheshire-cat grin. 'Laddie, can you call the waiter and ask for some Old River?'

Spencer poked his head through the dark barrier. Beyond the chalk semicircle, Pick Pocket Parlour was just as visible as before, and the sounds of people talking and glasses clinking were no longer muffled.

He caught the eye of a waiter and beckoned him over.

A short time later, the waiter returned with a dark-green bottle, labelled *Old River*, and Rabble made him clear all the glasses away.

'Sit back, everyone,' Rabble said.

He slowly poured the liquid in the bottle on to the tabletop, until it was a puddle the size of a large pot lid. 'Touch your wrist to the water,' Rabble told Mrs Pal.

She hesitated for a heartbeat before doing as asked. A moment later, the black line eased off her skin and into the small puddle.

'Ew!' Jelly yelped. 'It's growing!'

As the thin black line wafted back and forth in the water, it doubled, and then tripled in length, pushing the edges of the puddle outwards as it grew. Max would have poked an experimental finger into the water if Grandpa John hadn't held him back.

'Don't touch the water, children,' Mrs Pal warned.

'John, hold up the mirror,' said Rabble. 'And we need a light of some sort.'

'Here,' said Hedy, switching on the torch of her phone.

Rabble angled the beam into the reflective side of Grandpa John's mirror, and a pale silvery pattern shone down in wavy strokes and rippling circles that made the black line in the water twist excitedly.

'Keep it steady, John,' Rabble whispered.

The silvery pattern began to shift, clustering in three different spots. Growing quickly, the black line spread out, connecting each of the different clusters of light. They pulsed and small shapes rose up out of the Old River puddle, like very fine sculptures made of water. Deep in his chest, Spencer felt a reverberation, as though a massive, silent gong had been rung.

'Did you feel that?' Rabble said, looking about. 'You did, I can see it on all your faces. I think you can lower the mirror now, John.'

Even with the mirror lowered by Grandpa John's side, the clusters of light and small water shapes remained. Everyone leant in for a better look.

In one corner, the water sculpture seemed to be a rope bridge nestled amongst a collection of trees; beneath it glowed a symbol that looked like $\Pi$. The second corner had an underwater cave, dotted with pillars, and under that was the symbol $\phi$. The final corner was marked by a pier jutting from a shore, marked with the symbol $\approx$.

'Do you know what these symbols mean, Mr

Rabble?' Mrs Pal asked.

Rabble shook his head. 'But the shapes in the water, the bridge and the cave and the pier? I'll wager they're telling you about the locations.'

'Where are these places?'

The old man sucked at his teeth. 'Could be anywhere. If I had to guess, I'd say *that*,' he pointed to the bridge amongst the trees, 'is Puzzlewood, in England, near Gloucester. The bridge gives it away. I don't know where the other places are. What are you going to do? Are you going to tell the Sleight? This is significant.'

'Those fools?' Grandpa John grunted. 'I trust them about as far as I can throw them.'

'I wouldn't want Candice Harding finding out I'd called her a fool,' Rabble chuckled. 'Besides, the map being moored made a *noise*. We all felt it, so at least one of them will have felt it too. They'll know something was awoken, somewhere.'

'But they won't know it's Mrs Pal and me.'

Rabble snorted. 'Your optimism is charming, John.'

'We'll think about whether to tell the Sleight,' Mrs Pal said. 'Is there anything else we should know about the map?'

With a mischievous smile, he said, 'I could find a very wealthy buyer for it, if you'd like.'

'No need,' said Mrs Pal, pulling her sleeve down, 'but thank you.'

She held her fingers to the puddle of Old River. Immediately, the small water sculptures sank away into nothing and the pale silvery light disappeared. Rabble watched, eagle-eyed, as the black tattoo line curled through the water towards her fingertips and travelled, quick as lightning, up her hand.

'Do you feel it? The pull of the map?' asked Rabble, when no trace of the tattoo was left in the water.

Mrs Pal shook her head. 'It feels the same as before.'

'It unmoored itself,' Rabble frowned.

'But we just saw the completed map.'

Rabble rubbed his chin, thinking. 'John, you said your grandfather made the mirror?'

'Yes,' said Grandpa John, 'why?'

'I suspect crafty old Tsang Li Ming made *this* map work only for someone of his bloodline. Someone in your family.'

'Are you sure?' Mrs Pal asked. '*I* cultivated the map tattoo.' She sounded slightly cross.

'That's how it looks to me,' Rabble went on. 'I've

heard of those kinds of map moorings. Keeps people from accidentally stumbling upon it.'

'So, the map will live in Mr Sang, but not in me?'

'That's right.' Rabble smirked at Grandpa John. 'Bit old to be gallivanting around for powerful treasures, aren't you?'

'Quite,' said Grandpa John, slipping the mirror into his jacket pocket and signalling that it was time to go.

At Rabble's request, the children helped to rub the chalk marks away from the floor of the booth. As Spencer stepped out of their dark bubble to clean the last of the marks away, he bumped into a girl who was idling nearby with a lemonade. It was the girl from the Peacock Chamber earlier.

'Hello, Beatrice,' Rabble called amiably. 'Are you spying on me, or do you want to ask something?'

'I'll come back later, Mr Rabble,' she said. Spencer noticed Beatrice's eyes sweeping over the whole booth and everyone in it very carefully. But when she noticed him noticing *her*, she sauntered away to a far table where her father was sitting.

As they made their way to the door, Hedy whispered in Spencer's ear. 'Ha! I was right about the Theries here. Look!'

Spencer looked to where she pointed. A man with an angular face and a hawkish nose, dressed all in black, was leaning against a pillar and watching their group intently. He didn't bother to hide the fact that he was staring, and was too absorbed to notice a surreptitious hand reaching out towards his backpack from a nearby Therie painting.

Hedy seemed annoyed by the man's scrutiny. 'Looks like something's about to get pinched from his bag. Sucks to be him.'

It was as if the man in black had heard because, without looking behind him, he shifted his bag forwards, out of mischief's reach. Spencer had a foreboding sense that this wouldn't be the last they saw of him.

## CHAPTER 6

## THE OPENING CEREMONY

In the bustling main cavern, there seemed to be even more people than before. Many were heading towards the blocks of seating facing the centre stage.

'The opening ceremony will begin in fifteen minutes!' announced a voice from right above their heads, although when Hedy looked up she couldn't see any speakers.

'Can we watch?' Max asked.

Grandpa John didn't seem to hear, and his hand had absent-mindedly drifted to his jacket pocket where he kept the mirror.

It was Mrs Pal who answered Max. 'That's a fine idea. Let's find some seats.'

Max and Spencer dashed away with Jelly on their heels, warning them not to run too far ahead. As she hurried behind them, Hedy noticed a few teenagers hastening towards the stage with sashes across their chest that said *Fantastikhana Contestant*. People kept stopping them to offer congratulations and wish them luck in the competition. Besides the sashes, they looked like anyone else at her school; they wore normal clothes, had normal haircuts, had normal teenage complexions. *Do they all have gifts?* Hedy wondered.

'Hedy!' Max had nipped back to find her. 'Ice creams!' Grabbing her hand, he led her to the most curious-looking place yet – a huge round hut made of snow. 'Igloo!' he said.

*That can't be real*, Hedy thought, *it's not cold enough in this cavern for snow bricks to stay frozen*. The entrance was tall enough to walk through upright, and she followed Max inside where Spencer and Jelly moved through the small crowd, studying ice cream flavours.

'I want to try *Chomp Like a Chimp*,' Jelly declared.

'It says it's banana with ants, but I *think* the ants are just caramel chips.'

'They're not caramel chips,' said a strange voice nearby. Both Hedy and Jelly turned to look at the speaker. It was a boy of about sixteen, with thick blondish hair and a smattering of freckles across his nose.

'They're not?' Jelly said with a slight catch in her voice – a catch that Hedy instantly knew was not because of ants.

The boy just smiled in a way that made it hard to tell if he was joking or not, and wandered further around the snow hut to examine flavours. Hedy stifled a laugh at the way Jelly's eyes kept flicking in his direction.

'I'm having the *Quintuple Chocolate Folly*,' said Spencer. 'Hey Hedy, look up there. Did you bring your deck of cards?'

The sign hanging above the cashier read: *Opening Ceremony Special. Free orders for kids with magic tricks!*

Hedy grinned. 'Yeah, I brought them.'

'Can I borrow them? I'll try that trick where you always know the third card down the pack.'

'No, let Hedy do it,' Jelly insisted. 'She's better at it than you. You always muck up the last shuffle.'

'I don't *always* muck it up,' Spencer protested.

'OK, fine,' said Jelly, 'not always. Just mostly. Go on, Hedy, you're our best shot.'

Hedy slipped towards the cashier, deck of cards in hand. 'Four single cones, please,' she said.

'And are you taking advantage of our opening ceremony special?' asked the gawky young man.

She nodded and placed her deck of cards on the counter, sensing people around them pausing to watch. 'Could you shuffle the deck for me, please?'

The cashier did so, and Hedy then turned the pack over and showed them all to be in random order, memorizing the card that would later be revealed. Uncle Peter – Grandpa John's brother and also a former stage magician – had taught them this trick. It was one of her favourites because it didn't require too much sleight of hand. She had the cashier cut the deck in half and then went through the trick to its conclusion, correctly 'guessing' the third card down in one half of the pack.

Hedy was accustomed to chuckles of amazement and a few words of praise at that point. But the cashier looked at her, confused, and said, 'Oh, is that the end of your trick?'

'Well, yes. And I got the card right.'

He looked a bit uncomfortable. 'But it wasn't a *magic* trick. That was a bog's trick. Doesn't qualify for the special. Sorry.'

'What do you mean, "a bog's trick"?'

'Bog standard. Non-magician.'

*Bog standard.* Around them, onlookers were turning away, indifferent now it was clear that Hedy wasn't pulling off something actually magical.

The blond-haired boy from before had been watching. He stepped forward with a pitying look. 'Give them a discount for trying,' he suggested.

To Hedy's surprise, the cashier seemed pleasantly flustered at being spoken to by the blond-haired boy. 'Well, sure, since you asked, Cyrus.'

'Thanks,' Hedy mumbled, embarrassed. 'Actually, make that *three* ice creams.' She didn't feel like one herself any more.

'We did it, Mr Sang,' Hedy overheard Mrs Pal say as they all settled into their seats for the opening ceremony.

'Actually, *you* did it, Mrs Pal,' said Grandpa John. 'You figured out how to grow the unmoored map. I just happened to have the mirror. You're probably better than any other maker here.'

'You're not going to try finding it yourself, are you?' Mrs Pal asked.

'I don't think I have a choice.' Grandpa John didn't sound too unhappy about it. 'If it's going to be anyone, it'll have to be me. Like Rabble said, my crafty old grandfather seems to have made map moorings that will only work in someone of his bloodline.'

'But we don't know what the map leads to.'

'There is that,' Grandpa John frowned.

They fell silent when the lights of the cavern dimmed. A piper and a drummer walked onstage, counted out a beat and began to play a lively reel that quickly had people clapping in time. From behind the audience came the pitter-patter of many feet as a group of around forty children danced towards the stage.

At first it looked much like any other children's performance, with the smaller ones at the front and the older, taller ones at the back, all wearing matching costumes. But once all of them were onstage, the children began to cast charming illusions. When the young dancers all clapped in unison, the stage became a fairy glen with grassy hills rising up behind it. Proud parents in the audience cheered as the children flickered into fairies and danced among the spiralling stones. As the older children clicked their fingers, oversized toadstools popped up out of the ground for the smaller ones to clamber on to and dance on.

The next time the children clicked their fingers, the fairy glen changed to Stonehenge. They weaved in and out of the immense stone pillars, now looking as though they were dressed in long robes. Hedy had to stifle a giggle when, every now and then, some of the younger children didn't keep up their illusory costumes so well and their usual clothing appeared instead.

'I suspect following the map might be a bit like this dance,' Mrs Pal said to Grandpa John.

'What do you mean?' he asked.

'It might take you all around Britain.'

'Perhaps Rose would like a road trip with me.'

'On your motorbikes?' chuckled Mrs Pal. 'At your age?'

'Can I come with you?' whispered Hedy. Grandpa John ruffled her hair.

The children made their way through more famous landmarks: as soldiers marching across Tower Bridge, as kilted guards surrounding Edinburgh Castle, as outlaws in Sherwood Forest. Finally, the stage shimmered into a great lake and the children joined hands to become the Loch Ness Monster diving in and out of the water. Where the littlest kids couldn't keep up the illusion, it looked like they had been eaten by the Loch Ness monster and were peeking out from its insides.

'Better than your Christmas concerts, hey, Max?' Jelly said as the dance ended and the children bowed. She had a clog in one hand, and was trying to shake something out of it.

Max was too engrossed to be riled by his sister. He simply watched the stage for whatever was coming next, but to his disappointment it was only Candice.

'What a magnificent performance by our youngsters,' Candice said in her smooth voice. Although she didn't seem to have a microphone, her voice filled the cavern. 'And welcome to the Fantastikhana, everyone. We're very pleased to see so many gathered here, in beautiful Edinburgh. This year, we have more competitors than any Fantastikhana in thirty years!'

The audience cheered loudly.

'This event not only brings our families together from across the United Kingdom, it gives our younger generations a chance to learn from those with more experience. Over the next few days, we will be sharing knowledge, cementing friendships and celebrating our talented young prospects. We will find and nurture the leaders of tomorrow who will be able to keep our community safe. We are strong together, underground. Let us never forget that.'

'That's a bit over the top, surely,' Grandpa John muttered to Mrs Pal.

But when Hedy scanned the audience, their faces were all rapt and a few were nodding in agreement. To her consternation, she spotted the hawk-nosed man in black from Pick Pocket Parlour sitting a few rows behind them. He wasn't looking in her direction, but it seemed like he might have been, just a moment before she had turned around.

'So, let's celebrate our future,' Candice continued. 'On behalf of the Sleight, I welcome the competitors of this year's Fantastikhana!'

Candice reached up and plucked a glass of water out of nowhere. She tipped the glass, but instead of splashing to the floor, the water stopped short, hovering in the air about a foot from the ground. More and more water – many times more than a glass could hold – streamed out, and the hovering water began to rapidly grow. Within moments, it was as high as Candice's waist. She tossed the glass into the tumbling mass of water, and seconds later it had swelled to the size of a small truck.

Moving to the edge of the stage, Candice clicked her fingers. With a *boom*, the water exploded. But instead of soaking the audience, the water mass burst into enormous droplets that hung motionless in the air, frozen in place . . . and revealed between the floating beads of water were all the Fantastikhana competitors.

Hedy looked sidelong at Grandpa John, wondering if he could do what Candice had just done. Perhaps the same thought was on his mind, for his expression was one of shrewd appraisal, one showman sizing up another.

The audience clapped and cheered as Candice began to announce the competitors, from oldest to youngest. Soon, lined up at the front of the stage were two girls and a boy, all seventeen years old.

Before Candice could move on to the sixteen-year-old cohort, someone darted forward from the back of the stage. It was the blond-haired boy from the ice-cream hut. His voice rang throughout the cavern. 'Cyrus, sixteen!'

Jelly nudged Hedy in recognition. A loud murmur rose through the crowd. Overhead, the beads of water wobbled as Candice watched Cyrus take a bow; she looked furious. The audience all applauded, but this was different from their reactions to the first three contestants; Hedy could see people straining to get a better look at him, or turning to their neighbour and remarking upon his presence in the competition.

Jelly tugged on Hedy's sleeve, urging her to lean forwards; the couple in front of them were talking about the boy. 'It's a wonder Cyrus was able to get into the group without Candice finding out,' the woman was saying.

'There's no containing his power,' said the man. 'They should let him blow off some steam in the competition.'

'Everyone's heard rumours of what he can do. I wouldn't mind seeing some of it.'

The boy basked in the attention – it was as though everyone was there to see only him, as though he'd already won the competition. It wasn't until a stern word from Candice prompted him to line up with the three other teenagers that the applause petered out.

The other competitors all looked a little flummoxed as Candice announced them, their thunder stolen by Cyrus's interruption. On it went, until more than forty teenagers formed a line across the stage, the last to join them being the girl from the Peacock Chamber: Beatrice, thirteen years old.

'Her sash should say "Poltergeist Catcher",' Hedy whispered to Jelly, awed.

Candice swept her arm through the air and the giant beads of water rushed together, swirling into a waterspout that twisted and turned its way back into the glass in her hand. But suddenly there was a sharp cracking sound. A sizzle of blue light shot from Candice's hip, and the waterspout erupted in all directions. The first three rows of the audience were drenched, and shouts went up around the hall. From the look on Candice's face, it was entirely unplanned, and the pocket of her outfit was now nothing but a ragged, burnt hole.

Regaining her composure, Candice arced her arm through the air once more, and the water obediently streamed back into the glass from the saturated audience, leaving them perfectly dry. As the last of the water disappeared, the glass itself spun and shrank into her palm, then vanished.

'I apologize for the unexpected wash you all had,' she joked with an easy smile, ignoring the hole in her jacket. 'The first round will begin in two hours, and the Sleight wishes all our young competitors the best of luck. I declare the Fantastikhana open!'

Music started playing and the lights of the cavern came up again. The contestants filed off stage to find their families in the crowd, but Hedy noticed that Cyrus alone lingered onstage, looking as though he had nowhere to go.

'Maybe we should go and say hello to him,' Jelly whispered to Hedy. 'Does my hair look OK?'

But before Hedy could agree, or even tease her cousin about her blossoming crush on Cyrus, the lean-faced stranger in black appeared.

'Mr Sang, Mrs Pal,' he said. 'The Sleight would like to see you.'

## CHAPTER 7

## THE WRONG HANDS

The stranger said very little to them as they followed him through the crowd, besides advising that they were heading to the Peacock Chamber.

'Who is he?' Spencer asked, as he and Mrs Pal brought up the rear of their group.

The stranger paused, allowing a couple of people to cross their path. 'Call me Bess,' he said over his shoulder.

Grandpa John cast a worried look at Mrs Pal.

'A Bess?' Mrs Pal muttered with surprise.

Spencer leant in close to her. 'What's a Bess?'

'A treasure hunter,' said Mrs Pal. 'All treasure hunters take the title "Bess".'

Spencer studied Bess's back, thinking what an odd name it was for someone so imposing. 'What treasure do they hunt for?'

'Items of power.' Mrs Pal rubbed her wrist, where the edge of the tattoo map peeked out from her sleeve.

Bess knocked on the door of the Peacock Chamber and a muffled voice from inside called them in. Candice was at the head of the table, in the peacock chair, with a rather anxious-looking Ewan and two new people, one of them a man sporting a grand white moustache and a red tartan kilt. The man got to his feet.

'Hello, John,' he said. 'It's been a long time. I was glad to hear that Rose was returned.'

'No gladder than I, Morten,' Grandpa John said dryly as they shook hands.

The other newcomer, a young woman, stood as well. 'Hello, I'm Flora Maymon.' Her many silver bracelets clinked as she shook hands with them all.

'I totally *love* your headscarf,' Jelly gushed. 'Do any stalls here sell them?'

Flora patted her multi-coloured headscarf modestly.

'I'm sure you'll find more interesting things sold here than this. But if I see any, I'll get word to you.'

Mrs Pal seemed especially intrigued by the young woman. 'Are you any relation to Forrest Maymon?'

'He's my great-great uncle,' Flora nodded.

Spencer knew the name Forrest Maymon – a gold cast of his hands was kept by Mrs Pal at the Palisade. And with a second glance at Morten, he realized that his name sounded familiar as well. Anders and Morten, The Brothers of the Bifrost, had been stage magicians back when Grandpa John had been performing. Was this the same Morten? It was odd, Spencer thought, recognizing these people – or at least their names – like they were climbing out of history books.

As everyone took seats, Candice smiled at the children. 'How did you like the opening ceremony?'

'*Way* better than the concerts they put on at my school,' Spencer said. 'Especially the waterspout exploding at the end.' For a moment, he imagined himself pulling off a trick like that in front of everyone at his school, and maybe soaking the one or two kids who had been mean to him.

'That last part *wasn't* rehearsed,' said Candice, inspecting the hole in her jacket where her pocket should have been. 'I was too complacent about the spirit that that young girl had trapped. I should have put it in a strongbox, only I was too run off my feet. Now it's broken free and is floating around the Fantastikhana, bad luck waiting to happen.'

'We'll catch it soon enough,' said Morten. 'If it comes out of hiding to cause mischief, we'll detect it.'

The door suddenly thumped open, and in hurried Cyrus. Without a care for interrupting them, he declared, 'I've got it! Let me compete and I *promise* I won't try to win. Order the judges to give me the lowest score in every challenge. I just want to have fun while I still can.'

Candice got to her feet. 'Cyrus, can't you see we're in the middle of something?'

'But it's the perfect solution!' he barrelled on, ignoring her. 'A win-win for everyone. I mean, except for me, it'll be a non-win for me. And I'm all good with that.'

'We've been through this and it's not fair to the others,' said Candice firmly.

'I've got barely any time left!'

'You should be preparing for that with study, rather than tampering with the opening ceremony.'

'But—'

'Cyrus, we said no.'

At her unyielding manner, it seemed like actual light shining out of Cyrus dimmed with defeat. His shoulders slumped and he made for a chair in the corner, but Morten said, 'I think you'd better wait next door, lad.'

At last Cyrus seemed to appreciate that he had barged in on something. 'Why are they here?'

'None of your business,' said Candice.

He scowled. 'I'll be bogs like them before you guys teach me anything! Don't you think that's a waste?' He did his best to slam the door as he left, but either magic or clever design stopped it from banging.

Candice pinched the bridge of her nose. 'All right, where were we?'

'The boy had a point. Why *are* we here?' Grandpa John asked.

Considering her words carefully, Candice said, 'Rani, John, we became aware that something was awoken today. And we believe you have it.'

'What do you think we have?'

'A moored magician's map.'

'What makes you think we have it?'

'You were seen with it,' said Candice.

Grandpa John drummed his fingers on the table. 'Rabble. He's leakier than a broken sieve.'

'Not Rabble, actually. But we have our ways.' Candice smiled at Mrs Pal. 'It's quite remarkable, Rani. I haven't heard of anyone making a living map in a generation. How did you do it?'

Mrs Pal was silent for a long moment, until she finally said, 'Patience.' Everyone around the table waited for her to continue, but Spencer could tell that Mrs Pal was not going to reveal anything more and could out-wait them all.

'You have a map, but you don't know where or even *what* it's leading to.' Morten paused knowingly. 'But we might. You need our help.'

Grandpa John shook his head. 'I don't think so.'

'Come on, John, don't be so pig-headed. The map's awakening was felt,' said Morten. 'Whatever it leads to is important. You don't want to walk in blind.'

'Felt by many,' squawked a cockatoo.

Ewan tapped it. 'Hush, Chit.'

'Wanted by many,' added the other.

'Ewan, those damned parrots are driving me batty,' grumbled Morten. 'One day they're going to say something they shouldn't, at a time they shouldn't, and you'll lose them as well as your inheritance!'

Candice raised a placating hand. 'I don't think the birds have told John and Rani anything they don't know. Have they? I'm sure you *do* understand the magnitude of the map. And, as Morten said, it's not the sort of thing you'd tackle without first learning all you could. Perhaps you do already know what the map's quarry is.'

*She's so obvious!* Spencer thought. *Grandpa John's not going to fall for all that reverse-psychology stuff.*

But he and Mrs Pal did fall for it. Or at least, they seemed to wordlessly agree that it was a chance worth taking.

'Very well,' Grandpa John said. 'We'll show you. But we need some Old River water.'

At some unseen signal, an attendant appeared and was asked to bring a bottle of Old River. Within minutes, Mrs Pal was holding her wrist to the puddle on the tabletop, and the Sleight watched, mesmerized, as the black tattoo line snaked off her skin into the water. Grandpa John then pulled the mirror from his jacket pocket and angled it to catch a beam and reflect it into the puddle.

Every single Sleight member leant forwards as the silvery reflection clustered and three miniature water sculptures rose out of the liquid. Spencer felt that deep shake in his chest again.

'That's it,' Flora smiled. 'It *is* what I thought.'

'How do you know?' Candice asked.

'Those symbols!' Flora exclaimed, pointing to the $\Pi$, $\phi$ and $\approx$ shapes in the light.

Grandpa John let the mirror drop, but the map remained shimmering on the table. 'What do the symbols mean?'

'Frame, stone and thread. They signify the three parts of Verdandi's Loom.'

Flora's words made Grandpa John gape like a fish. Mrs Pal gripped the edge of the table until her knuckles turned white.

'What's Verdandi's Loom?' Jelly asked. 'You mean like a weaving loom?'

'Verdandi's Loom!' cawed Chit.

Chat bobbed up and down on Ewan's shoulder. 'Verdandi's Loom weaves through time!'

Watching Ewan rub his face in mortification, Spencer suspected the birds were repeating what they had overheard the Sleight discussing.

Hedy asked, 'How can it weave through time?'

'The full history of Verdandi's Loom is lost,' Flora explained, 'but it was created to make changes to the past, suspend the present, or change the future.'

'Every one of those options is dangerous,' Grandpa John added darkly.

'John,' said Candice, 'I know you look down your nose at us, but it just so happens that we're in violent agreement. Manipulating time can indeed be perilous. Obviously your own grandfather shared that opinion, because Tsang Li Ming was one of those who split up Verdandi's Loom and helped to hide it. That's why your family has the mirror that moors the magician's map.'

Everybody's eyes fell upon the small mirror in Grandpa John's hand. *My great-great-grandfather held that once*, Spencer thought, feeling the tug of a mysterious history. *And he was more than just a stage magician.*

'I'm glad we're agreed,' Grandpa John said. 'Although it leaves little more to say. You don't want the Loom floating around, and nor do I.'

'Very good, John,' said Candice, 'which is why we ask that you give the map to the Sleight.'

'You're joking,' he scoffed.

'I'm quite serious.'

Grandpa John shoved the mirror back into his jacket pocket. 'The map doesn't belong to you. Besides, it's as much Mrs Pal's as it is mine.'

'Rani,' said Candice to Mrs Pal, 'we respect your abilities. And to be frank, it's part of the problem. We can't have you getting the Loom and selling it to any highest bidder out there.'

'I'm not some black-market arms dealer,' Mrs Pal said, as irritated as Spencer had ever seen her.

'You're one of the busiest traders out there,' Morten pointed out. 'And John's not your only customer.'

'I would never sell the map from under him!' Mrs Pal was actually offended now.

'We simply feel,' said Candice, 'that Verdandi's Loom needs to be kept out of the wrong hands.'

Grandpa John snorted. 'There isn't much that will convince me the hands of the Sleight are the right ones.' He smiled grimly at Candice. 'Besides, the map won't work in you. The map only keeps its moorings in me.'

'You mean, in Tsang Li Ming's bloodline,' Candice corrected him. 'Ewan?'

Too late, Spencer, Grandpa John and the rest of

them realized that Candice meant for Ewan – their cousin a few times removed – to take the map that glistened in the puddle. Ewan threw Grandpa John a remorseful look as he extended his trembling hand towards the tabletop. Grandpa John reached out to stop him but gasped – Morten was holding him back from getting in the way.

'No!'

The shout came from Hedy. Faster than the reluctant Ewan, she thrust her own hand into the pool of Old River water that rippled with the magician's map.

## CHAPTER 8

### STOWAWAY

Sight and sound faded. The only thing Hedy knew was the sensation of the map markings surging up her hands, arms, everywhere. It was like the map was looking for countless spots to anchor itself, spreading as fast as wildfire. And the feeling wasn't confined to her skin; it seemed to be sinking down into her very bones as well.

At last, the Peacock Room sharpened back into focus. Although Hedy felt that she'd been oblivious for hours, it must have only been a moment, for everyone was exactly where they had been, but staring at her, dumbstruck.

Spencer was the first to break the silence. 'Tattoos? You're going to be in *so* much trouble with Mum and Dad!'

Hedy lifted her right hand, then pulled her sleeve back. Black swirling lines snaked from her fingers all the way up her arm. A silvery cluster, like the reflection from the magic mirror, sat near the crook of her elbow. Although she couldn't wrestle her sleeve any higher, she could feel the map tattoos continuing up her shoulder, around her neck and . . . she touched her left cheek.

'Is it on my face?' she asked Jelly.

Jelly grimaced. She reached out a finger to show Hedy where the markings were, but then thought better of touching them. 'Only on the left side.'

*What have I done?* Hedy thought. She felt like the floor was dropping out from beneath her.

Grandpa John shook off Morten's grip and stalked around the table. That familiar crease of worry had appeared between his eyebrows. 'Hedy, are you hurt?'

'It doesn't hurt,' she said.

He relaxed just a tiny bit. 'What were you thinking?'

'I wanted to keep the map for you.'

Grandpa John drew her into a hug that conveyed rebuke, gratitude and regret all at once. Then he rounded on Candice and Morten, furious. 'This is your fault.'

'Wrong,' Candice snapped. 'If you'd given us the map willingly, your granddaughter wouldn't have made such a rash decision.'

Even Mrs Pal bristled at that. 'I think what you actually meant to say was, if you hadn't tried to *bully* us, she wouldn't have made such a decision.'

'Time out, everyone,' Flora interrupted. 'What's done is done. Hedy, you said it doesn't hurt. That's good. Can you tell us how you are feeling?'

Hedy lifted her marked hand and clenched it into a fist. 'I can feel that they're there. And I feel like I'm being pulled.'

'Pulled how?'

'Like there's a big magnet out there somewhere, trying to pull me towards it.' She pointed, not having a clue as to what point of the compass it was. 'That way somewhere.'

Flora smiled ruefully. 'Well, the good news is that you are the bearer of a real, living moored map.'

'Great,' Hedy mumbled.

'Hedy, you shouldn't be saddled with this,' said Grandpa John. 'You can let the map go back into the water.' The puddle of Old River quivered invitingly on the tabletop.

'But the map is yours,' Hedy said, 'and they're trying to take it from you.'

'I won't take it,' Ewan declared abruptly. He squared his shoulders as Candice glared at him across the table. 'Not without Mr Sang's – John's – permission. It wasn't right of you to ask me, Candice.'

When no one said anything, Hedy tentatively reached her hand to the small pool of water. Everybody seemed to hold their breath. Moments ticked by. Nothing. The map tattoos obstinately stayed in her skin.

Candice beckoned Bess and whispered to him. He hurried out of the room.

'I think it might be best if the children wait next door,' she said to Grandpa John, 'so that we can discuss what to do.'

'Even me?' Hedy frowned.

'You'll be more comfortable in there. Ewan, will you escort them, please?'

*

The next room was occupied already by Cyrus. He was stretched out on a leather settee, his legs dangling over one of its arms, but Hedy thought he had the posed air of someone who had leapt on to the settee moments ago to appear nonchalant. When he caught sight of her and the mark on her cheek, he sat up, eyes wide.

'What happened?' he asked.

'These kids will be waiting in here while the grown-ups talk things over,' Ewan said evasively, before introducing them all.

Cyrus got to his feet. 'Can I go in yet?'

'Best sit tight until Candice calls you.'

The five of them stared at each other awkwardly as Ewan closed the door behind him. Finally, Cyrus waved a hand at the tables and chairs scattered through the room. 'You can sit anywhere you want.' Spencer and Max plonked themselves on the rug in front of the fireplace, where a fire crackled away.

'We saw you onstage before,' Jelly said, 'in the opening ceremony.'

Cyrus grinned. 'I wasn't supposed to be in it.'

'Why not?'

'Because I'd probably win without trying too hard. They don't think it's fair to other kids.' He pointed at

Hedy's cheek. 'What happened? You didn't have that before.'

Hedy hesitated, unsure how much she should reveal.

'It's a living map,' Jelly blurted out. 'Kind of a family heirloom. Uncle John – he's my grandad's brother – he had this mirror that was handed down to him from *their* grandfather. And Mrs Pal grew this unmoored map. And they found out how to make the two things work together to make it a *moored* map and it shows the way to—'

At a sharp nudge from Hedy, Jelly caught herself and stopped. 'To something,' she finished lamely.

Hedy's secretive manner didn't seem to bother Cyrus. 'You're right to be cautious about who you tell stuff to,' he said. He rummaged around in a cupboard as though he was all too familiar with waiting here, and produced three packets of biscuits. 'May as well feast while we're waiting for the adults to figure out what they do with us next.'

His tone was bright on the surface, but there was a note of reproach underneath it. Hedy found herself agreeing. 'Yeah, it's not fair,' she said softly. 'I should have been allowed to stay in there, since I've ended up with the tattoos.'

The girls sat down at a table and Jelly, complaining about her clog, bent down to inspect it for the umpteenth time. The rustle of biscuit packets immediately had Spencer and Max scurrying over.

Hedy mulled over Cyrus's interruption in the Peacock Chamber and asked, 'What did you mean before? When you said you've got barely any time left?'

Max looked Cyrus up and down. 'Are you sick? Are you going to die?'

'*Max!*' the others all hissed.

'No,' said Cyrus slowly, 'I've sort of got a condition, but I'm not ill.'

With a sudden snort of surprise, Jelly held up her clog. A little tell-tale bulge popped out of the heel. 'It's a Woodspy!' she cried out.

'A Woodspy?' Cyrus said blankly.

'Our grandfather's got three of them at his house,' Spencer explained. 'They can move through anything wooden – like floors and doorframes and things like that.'

Jelly's surprising clumsiness, ever since they had entered the tunnel back in Stradmoor, now made sense.

'He stowed away in your shoe all the way from Grandpa John's,' Hedy smiled. 'I bet it's the smallest one. He's always been the most curious.'

'You sneaky little . . .' Jelly shook the clog hard. 'You've been turning me into such a bumble-footed loser all day, tripping me up like that. Is it just one of you, or have I been taking the whole family on a cruise all this time?'

The Woodspy shrank into the clog, ashamed.

'Don't yell at the baby,' Max scolded his sister. 'It didn't know it was doing anything wrong.' To Cyrus, he added, 'Don't worry, they're friendly.'

Cyrus nodded solemnly. 'All right, I won't worry.'

'But they do steal little things and hide them in the floor sometimes,' said Spencer, 'like toys and socks.'

'And they helped you spy on some of Uncle John's secret stuff,' Jelly said. She waggled her clog, hinting.

'So, do you think,' Cyrus mused, 'that your Woodspy could listen in on next door and tell you what they say?'

'They don't talk,' Hedy said. She thought for a moment. 'But maybe it could help *us* listen?'

In a heartbeat, the five of them were huddled by the wall between their room and the Peacock Chamber.

'Little one,' Hedy said to Jelly's clog, 'we need to know what the grown-ups are saying next door. Do you think you could open up a tiny little tunnel so that we can listen?'

The Woodspy wobbled excitedly in the shoe: *Yes*.

She placed the clog on the wooden floor. A barely discernible round lump flowed out of the heel and down into the floorboard before disappearing beneath the skirting board.

A minute or two ticked by.

'I hope it doesn't get lost,' Jelly muttered. At Cyrus's quizzical look, she said, 'They're like little kids. They get a bit distracted.'

And then near the wall, a tiny, dark knot in the wood opened up, no more than a centimetre across. They all froze.

'Thank you for joining us, Rabble,' Candice was saying.

The Woodspy had done it! Hedy lifted a finger to her lips, warning the boys to stay quiet. If they could hear the grown-ups, the reverse might be true as well.

'I didn't have much choice,' Rabble complained. 'Not with Bess looming over me. D'you know what he's like? A great black crow staring at you like you owe him money.'

'You don't want to know what I look like to people who owe me money,' said Bess.

'Rabble, as you already know,' said Candice, 'John and Rani here have awoken a living map. In a rather unfortunate turn of events, the map tattoos have ended up on John's granddaughter.'

Rabble spluttered. 'How did you manage that?'

'Best we don't get into that right now,' Flora jumped in, anxious to head off another quarrel. 'But we need your help. You probably know more about living maps than anyone here. Can the map be removed from the girl?'

There was a tutting noise and footsteps as Rabble paced. 'They say the only way to rid yourself of a moored map is to find what you're seeking. The pull of it will only grow stronger in her.'

Silence fell on the room next door and all four of the children stared at Hedy. She swallowed hard, her mouth suddenly feeling dry as dust.

'Do you know what you're seeking?' Rabble asked eventually.

His question was met with even more silence,

which was answer enough.

'Well, if you've nothing else to share with me, I'll be off. All right with you, black crow?' The last tart question must have been directed at Bess.

Once Rabble had left the Peacock Chamber, Grandpa John burst out, 'I can't believe Rabble is really the best there is, the most knowledgeable on living maps! There must be a way to extract it from Hedy. Mrs Pal?'

'You know that if I could think of a way, Mr Sang, I would tell you,' said Mrs Pal softly.

'John,' said Candice, 'you'd better start preparing your granddaughter for a journey.'

'What do you mean?'

'Bess is very experienced—'

A chair scraped back angrily. 'She's not going anywhere with this *hunter*, this—'

Hedy felt Jelly's arm slip around her shoulders comfortingly. She found her knuckles were pressed anxiously to her mouth.

'You can go with them, John,' Flora said soothingly. 'If it would make you feel better. That would be all right, wouldn't it, Candice?'

'We can allow it,' said Candice. 'On the crystal-clear

understanding that Verdandi's Loom will be brought back to the Sleight. It can't stay in that crumbling house of yours, John, nor can we trust that it will be safe at the Palisade.'

'Why would you think I'd feel better handing it over to you, wallowing in your pathetic abilities like rats underground?' Grandpa John's voice was so loud that Hedy thought they might have heard him even without the Woodspy's help. 'Not one of the Sleight was of any help finding Rosie. My own grandchildren, with no training or ability whatsoever, were the ones who solved it all.'

'What happened to Rose was not our fault!' Candice snapped.

'We're not handing it over to you.'

'You'll have to,' said Candice, her voice steelier than ever. 'You won't be able to leave the Fantastikhana until you agree.'

## CHAPTER 9

### WHISKER WISH

Grandpa John and Mrs Pal were both tight-faced when they arrived to collect the children. At a gesture from Ewan, Cyrus hurried to the door. 'That was fun,' he said. 'I'll catch you guys in the main cavern sometime, OK?'

Spencer and Max giggled at Jelly's captivated expression.

'What are we doing now?' Hedy asked.

'We're leaving,' Grandpa John said brusquely. 'Gather your things.'

'Leaving this room or leaving the Fantastikhana?'

Spencer asked.

'The Fantastikhana.'

'What?' Spencer yelped, dismayed. 'But we haven't had a chance to see anything yet! Not proper stuff like the tournament and workshops and stalls!'

'You won't be able to leave, John, sorry,' Ewan mumbled, giving Spencer a small lift of hope.

But Grandpa John was adamant. 'Just take us out to the exit, please, Ewan.'

As they walked through the main cavern, many of the passers-by regarded the map tattoo on Hedy's face curiously, although no one remarked on it. Not within earshot, anyway. As they got closer to the great revolving door through which they'd arrived, Hedy suddenly grew very pale, making the black markings on her face stand out more than ever. She wilted against Jelly.

'What's wrong?' Grandpa John said, moving to her side to hold her up.

'It hurts to try and go that way,' she said.

Mrs Pal looked at Grandpa John grimly. 'Candice wasn't bluffing. They must have put a ward on the exit. They're not going to let Hedy leave.'

They retreated from the cavern exit. With every step, Hedy revived a little more, and soon enough she told them she felt quite normal again.

'Now what do we do?' said Grandpa John.

With a tap of her walking stick, Mrs Pal said, 'Let's think while we look around the Fantastikhana.'

In Spencer's opinion, the buzzing main cavern was the perfect place to distract Hedy from the map markings, which weren't really *that* obvious if you didn't look at the left side of her face, and if she'd stop fussing with her hand.

Competitors were being shepherded to assembly areas, many of them pulling along boxes of equipment on small wagons. Encouraging parents watched them line up while bored siblings tugged on the parents' sleeves, impatient to investigate the stalls along the sides of the cavern.

The stalls had so many intriguing things to look at: handheld windmills that changed colour and played a tune as one blew on them; toadstool-growing kits which, the stall-keepers told young children, would entice small brownies to the garden; a pencil that never needed sharpening and turned any colour you wished.

Spencer used some of his pocket money to buy Mum and Dad a Scottish souvenir: a wooden rod that the Scots used to make porridge, called a spurtle. 'Aye, that spurtle is magic,' the shopkeeper assured him, popping it into a paper bag. 'Makes anyone who eats the silky-smooth porridge love and treasure the cook who used it.'

'It does not,' Ewan scoffed. 'Jake, you're not even Scottish.'

'What's that got to do with it?'

'Well, I know for a fact it doesn't work to conduct a love enchantment. Unless you sold me a dud.'

'I can't help that you're a mighty poor cook, Ewan!'

As the pair teased one another, Max and Jelly scooted up to Spencer, holding a small glass jar.

'What's that?' Max asked him, pointing at the spurtle. 'A fat wand?'

'It's a spurtle. It stirs porridge,' Spencer explained.

Max pulled a face. 'Boring!'

'Well, it's magic, so it's not *that* boring,' Spencer retorted crossly. 'What do *you* have?'

'Fur-growing ointment. For Doug!'

'You know that girl from the Peacock Chamber?' said Jelly. 'Well, she was just over there with the most amazing bunny rabbit. It had this incredible beard and moustache, so we asked her about it and she told us which stall was selling the ointment that makes its beard grow. Look, there's the rabbit!'

Spencer turned to where Jelly was pointing, and spotted the fluffiest rabbit that he had ever seen. Its fur was pale grey, and around its face was a mane of rabbit wool that had been styled into a long beard and a twirly moustache. Its owner was indeed Beatrice, and she was intently studying Hedy, who was at the next stall buying a hooded sweatshirt.

A protective impulse came over Spencer and he strolled pointedly to Hedy's side. Hedy sensed his presence, and when she followed his gaze to catch Beatrice still staring, the girl looked abashed at last. 'Sorry,' she said, 'I was just looking at your . . . tattoos. I haven't seen anything like them before.'

'Oh,' Hedy said, her hand flitting to her cheek. 'They're sort of an accident.'

'What do they do?' asked the girl.

Grandpa John caught Hedy's eye and shook his head, warning her not to give away anything.

'Um, I don't know yet,' Hedy answered. 'Or not exactly.'

Beatrice's father smiled. 'Are you competing? Did you get them to help you in your challenges?'

Hedy shook her head. 'No, we're just watching the tournament.'

'So, is it a *gift*, is that what they call it?' he asked. 'We're sort of new to all this, we're not really on top of all the magician's lingo and all that. When I say *sort of new*, I mean totally and utterly new. This is our first year, isn't it, Bea? Oh, my name's Ned.'

'Dad, we'd better get back to the staging area,' Beatrice said, starting to look embarrassed.

'You should come watch Bea's challenge!' he went on eagerly. He waved a finger at Spencer. 'Put your hand up and she might call you up onstage!'

At that moment, Mrs Pal ambled over and the father's friendly manner faltered. 'Er, time for us to go,' he stammered, and the mortified Beatrice dragged him off to where the competitors were gathering.

'People think you have a *gift*!' Jelly said, nudging Hedy with her elbow jokingly. 'If I'd known that, I would've put *my* hand in the water.'

Hedy pulled the sweatshirt on, lifted the hood up over her head and tugged the sleeves, which were printed with FANTASTIKHANA in bold lettering, right down to her knuckles. 'Maybe I can be home-schooled for the next five years,' she said darkly.

'Come on, the tattoos aren't *that* bad.'

'I know you're just trying to make me feel better. But it's not like having a cute daisy on my ankle or something. There's no way I'll survive school with these.'

Jelly seemed determined to console Hedy, but then something else caught her attention. 'Max, what are you doing?'

Max guiltily whipped his hands from his head. The small jar of ointment was open in his hand.

'Did you just put that stuff on your scalp?'

'I want to see if I'll grow fur with my hair,' Max said with an innocent smile.

Spencer peered at his bogey-obsessed cousin's face, which was shiny around the nostrils. 'You rubbed your nose with that hand too, didn't you?'

With a vexed squeak, Jelly began wiping at Max's nose with a tissue, while Spencer and Hedy fell into fits of giggles. *At least she's not so down now*, Spencer thought. 'Can we go and watch that girl in the tournament?' he asked.

'Why, because you want to go up onstage with her?' Hedy teased.

'People will be watching the kids doing tricks there,

rather than staring at you,' he pointed out. 'Come on, let's get seats close to the front!'

The forty-two Fantastikhana competitors all had to choose a number of challenges to complete throughout the tournament. Each challenge had a concept as a starting point, and competitors were free to devise their own interpretation of that concept, one that showed their skill and flair in the best light. 'Stage Magic Traditions' was the central idea for this particular challenge.

One by one, the teenage magicians worked their tricks onstage, captivating Spencer and the others. There was a small girl who used a magic guillotine to both cut off her hand and stitch it back on. She was followed by a brawny boy who had every single member of the audience and judges' panel find a coin behind their ear. (Unfortunately, the judges wouldn't let anyone keep them due to rules against bribery, and all the coins had to be made to vanish by the young magician.)

Next was a confident boy who played on the well-used levitation trick of stage magicians, although his didn't go quite as planned. He levitated all of the judges smoothly, but then suffered a fit of sneezing which, for a split second, sent a fizz of blue light up into the air. One of the judges was tipped out of his chair and crashed to the ground, while another was stuck up in the air. The boy, even once recovered from his sneezing, couldn't seem to bring her down again. She had to judge the remainder of the challenge from five metres off the ground.

When Beatrice came onstage, her only prop was a magician's black top hat. 'This hat,' she announced in a loud but somewhat stilted tone, 'is empty, as you can see.' To prove it, she gave the hat a hearty shake, then showed its unoccupied insides to the audience. 'If only I could grant a Whisker Wish . . . I'd wish for my pet rabbit, Leo, just so I could pull him out of the hat, and prove that I'm a real magician. Oh! What's this?'

The hat had started wriggling in her hands. With a stagey air of surprise, Beatrice reached a hand into her hat and scooped out her bearded, moustached rabbit. 'It's Leo!' she cried. The rabbit's nose twitched in the middle of his chubby bunny cheeks, provoking squeals and 'aww' noises all through the crowd.

'Weak!' someone yelled as Beatrice put Leo into a large cage that someone had rolled on behind her. All heads jerked around, and the heckler stood up. It was

Beatrice's own father. 'Any magician can pull a rabbit out of a hat. What else have you got?'

Beatrice smiled. The interruption was obviously planned between them. 'All right, I'll prove the power of the Whisker Wish again. Someone else can wish for their pet. Are there any takers?'

Half expecting this, Spencer shot his arm into the air as fast as lightning.

'You've got one here!' Beatrice's dad called out.

The next thing Spencer knew, he was trotting down the aisle to the steps that led up to the stage, blushing at all the eyes upon him. 'Go Spence!' he heard Hedy and his cousins shout.

'Um, hello,' Beatrice said, shaking his hand. Stage patter didn't appear to be her strong suit. 'What's your name?'

'Spencer.'

'OK, Spencer, do you have a pet at home?'

'Sort of, yes.'

'Well, I want you to hold the hat like this – that's it – and think of your pet at home.'

'Can I think of two?' Spencer asked.

Beatrice was a little thrown by the question at first but after a moment's thought, she said, 'Uh, sure.

Yes. So, close your eyes, think of them, picture them in your mind from the tops of their heads to their feet and tails – if they have tails – and then when they're clear in your mind, say, "Whisker Wish be granted".

Spencer closed his eyes, concentrated very hard and repeated, 'Whisker Wish be granted.' He opened his eyes. The hat was lifeless in his hands. Beatrice chewed her lip and nervously fidgeted with something in her pocket.

'Should I feel something?' he muttered under his breath.

A sudden crackle of blue light fizzled around the interior of the hat, and then the hat itself lurched out of Spencer's grasp. The blue of that light – which had flashed out of Candice's pocket, and quite possibly done something to the sneezing levitation boy earlier – reminded Spencer uncomfortably of Albert Nobody causing trouble at Hoarder Hill.

On the stage floor, the hat strained and stretched, like something was pushing inside a balloon.

'Do you have Great Danes or something?' Beatrice asked. She eyed the judges uneasily as her hat rolled across the stage, distending even more.

'No,' Spencer replied. It seemed a bit late to tell her what pets he *had* been imagining.

The hat was huge and misshapen now. Finally, Spencer heard something from inside it that convinced him Beatrice had indeed pulled off some remarkable magic.

'Stop poking me in the rump with your blinking pointy pointers!'

'Then trundle faster, you corpulent brute. Walking behind your backside is no treat for my nose, I can tell you.'

The entire audience held its breath, then burst into applause as a brown bear and a tall stag emerged from the magician's hat.

'I say, Douglas,' said Stan, as chuffed by the cheers as if he had accomplished the magic feat himself. Stamping his legs, he added, 'Look, I have hooves!'

## CHAPTER 10

## UNDERTOW

Bringing Doug and Stan through the Whisker Wish was astonishing enough to secure Beatrice the highest score for that round of the tournament. She came to thank Spencer as soon as the challenge was over.

'I was expecting you to have a dog and maybe a hamster,' she said, jiggling whatever was in her pocket.

Although Beatrice was talking to Spencer, Hedy found herself the subject of Beatrice's intense stare again. She pulled up her hood self-consciously, thinking, *This is what life will be like if I don't get rid of the map tattoos.*

After asking Hedy's name, Beatrice unexpectedly held out a cute cloth-covered hair clip. 'Would you like one of these? I was given some at one of the stalls. It'd match your top.'

'Um, sure. Thank you,' said Hedy. The girl was odd, but Hedy didn't want to seem rude.

'How are you allowed to have a bear and a deer as pets?' Beatrice asked her.

Spencer jumped in. 'They're more our friends than pets, really. And they're usually a bear rug and a stuffed deer head.'

As they chatted, Hedy's mind wandered. The pull of the map inside her was growing, but she didn't want to worry Grandpa John about it – not while he was trying to make a decision about what to do. Instead she buried her face in Doug and Stan's fur, taking comfort in their familiar voices and the very unfamiliar feel of muscle and bone beneath their pelts.

'Good grief, look at that,' fussed Stan.

Doug rumbled, 'You'll have to find out a way to get rid of it before we go back to the real world, or it'll cause a right stir.'

Hedy glanced up, thinking they were talking to her.

But instead everyone was gawking at Max, whose hair seemed to have grown five centimetres in the time they had been watching the tournament. He was also proudly patting a moustache that had sprouted on his face.

Hedy began to chuckle, momentarily letting go of her worries about the map tattoos. 'I'm glad you're both here.'

'So am I, cub, now that I'm getting over the shock of it. Look at the heft of this paw,' said Doug.

'I feel like I could run around the world a few times,' said Stan, prancing.

'You know what else we've got? Stomachs.' Doug sniffed the air. 'And mine's feeling empty.'

As Ewan led them around the cavern to his favourite food stall, their motley group unsurprisingly captured a lot of attention. *Animals, moustachioed boy, tattooed girl*, Hedy thought, *we're like a travelling circus.*

'Tattie scones,' Ewan said, handing out hot potato flatbread as they settled under a stand of trees. 'This is exactly what I used to eat when I was young and walking around the Fantastikhana with my parents. That was the best part of the competition for me.'

'Did you ever win?' Max asked.

'No,' Ewan confessed. 'I'm not what you'd call a very gifted magician. A bit of an embarrassment to the family, really.'

'Dove wouldn't fly from the cape,' Chit said.

'Rabbit almost squashed in the hat,' added Chat.

'Couldn't levitate.'

'Nearly cut that woman in half!'

'Never got the right card to appear.'

'OK, OK, they get the picture,' Ewan sighed.

Jelly nudged Hedy. 'Shall we go and say hi?' Not far away, at a windowed booth about two metres tall, stood Cyrus. Inside the booth was a mannequin of a woman with an old-fashioned typewriter. There was a small family waiting to use the booth after Cyrus, and they seemed to be whispering about him.

'He looks like he's in the middle of something,' Hedy said. 'Ewan, what's that booth?'

'Oh, that's Maureen,' said Ewan. 'She's a fortune-teller machine.'

There was no turban or crystal ball or glittery rings adorning the mannequin. Instead, she was dressed in a neat old-fashioned suit and had her fingers poised over the typewriter.

'She doesn't look very fortune-teller-y.'

'Well,' said Ewan, 'legend has it that Maureen was a mannequin in an old department store and a window dresser discovered she could tell fortunes. No one wanted to make any changes to her in case it affected her abilities. That's why she's not dressed like some gypsy seer. Look, there she goes.'

Cyrus had leant close to the booth and whispered a question, prompting Maureen to jerkily type a message on her typewriter. Then the mannequin tore the paper off and fed it through a gap in the window. Whatever was on the slip of paper seemed to disappoint Cyrus: he stuffed it in his pocket, slumping.

Ewan went on, 'She usually doesn't tell you very *interesting* fortunes. But she's quite accurate, according to scholars who have studied her.'

'Have *you* ever asked Maureen for your fortune?' Jelly asked.

'When I was around seventeen, I asked what my life would be like as a grown man.'

'What did she tell you?'

'She said I'd be cleaning up a lot of bird droppings.' Ewan tried to ignore the children's mirth. 'She's been known to tell people they'd be dead and buried in five or ten years' time. And the truth is, many people don't really want to know that.'

'I want to try it out,' Jelly said seriously, 'but I *don't* want to hear that I'm going to be pushing up daisies in a few years.'

'Can I try it?' Max asked, already on his feet and making a beeline for the booth.

'Fine.' Jelly grabbed Hedy's hand. 'Now we have an excuse to say hi.'

Cyrus had begun walking in the opposite direction but, at Jelly's call, he turned. He looked lost and troubled and it took him a moment to force a smile.

'Did you get bad news?' Hedy couldn't help asking. She could sense the family next in line for the booth studying them, although she wasn't sure if they were curious about the marks on her face or about Cyrus.

'Nothing surprising. She gives me the same fortune every time.' Cyrus pointed at Max's moustache. 'What happened?'

They told him about the fur-growing ointment as they waited for the family to finish up with Maureen. None of them seemed as downcast about their slips of paper as Cyrus had been. As they moved away, both parents murmured hello to Cyrus, while their children gawked at him as though he were famous.

'Do you know them?' Jelly asked when they had left.

'Not really. People think they know me, though.'

'Why?'

'Something that happened when I was little.' He stepped forward and gave Max a coin. 'Here, get a fortune on me. I hope it's better than mine.'

Max dropped the coin in the slot, then stood on tiptoe to speak into the little funnel of the booth. 'Will my hair keep growing like this for ever?'

Jelly groaned. 'What a waste of a question!'

Inside the booth, Maureen's typewriter went *clacketty-clack*, and a few moments later the mannequin swiped the top strip of her paper off the roller and fed it out.

'You will be bald by the age of fifty-seven,' Max read, crestfallen. He reached up to pat his ever-growing hair protectively.

As Spencer and Jelly debated who would go next and what they would ask, Hedy began to feel strange. Everything was fading away, everything except the pull of the map markings. It was like a beachside current turning into a powerful undertow, dragging whatever it could out to sea. Without realizing it, she began to follow that pull. What a relief it was not to resist it any more! She mindlessly stumbled towards wherever the map was guiding her, stepping out of people's way when they crossed her path.

Gentle teeth gripped her hand, startling Hedy from her trance. It was Doug. Looking behind, she saw a corridor of astonished people who had hurriedly cleared the way as the bear had chased her. Grandpa John hastened towards them. 'Where were you going?' he asked, worried.

'I – I don't know,' Hedy stammered.

'Is it the map?'

She nodded. Further ahead was nothing but brick-work in the cavern wall.

'Don't go anywhere without me,' said Grandpa John, patting her shoulder. 'We'll leave the Fantastikhana as soon as we can, go home and figure this out.'

After they'd eaten, Ewan said he'd take them to their hotel. To everyone's surprise, Chit and Chat alighted from Ewan's shoulders to hang upside down from Stan's antlers. As they walked through the main cavern, many of the passers-by seemed to recognize the birds, calling out things like, 'Afternoon, Chit and Chat! Given away any professional secrets today?' and 'Haven't you fallen off your mortal perches yet, you chatterboxes?' It all caused Stan to strut with a rather self-important lift to the head.

'Stan, you look nuttier than a squirrel's winter store,' growled Doug.

'You're just jealous,' said the stag.

'Jealous of a couple of barmy blabbermouths dangling off your antlers?'

'Well, what about you, lumbering along with a human mushroom sprouting from your back?'

Max, who had cajoled Doug into giving him a ride on his back, patted his hair indignantly. 'I'm not a mushroom!'

'Your hair is so out of control you can barely see,' said Jelly. She took the hair clip that Beatrice had given Hedy and clipped a patch of Max's hair back from his forehead. 'There, that's better.'

There was a funny expression on Cyrus's face as he stared at the hair clip, but he said nothing. He and the girls dropped back to the tail end of their group. With her hood up, Hedy felt shielded from curious eyes, but even better deflection was Cyrus himself, for he drew the wide-eyed looks and murmurs of passing strangers more than Stan, the birds and Max put together.

'What happened back there, when you walked off?' Jelly asked Hedy.

Hedy tried to explain the feeling of being drawn along by the map, of not being aware of her surroundings until Doug had stopped her as she faced the bricks of the cavern perimeter.

'I know where it was taking you,' said Cyrus.

'Where?'

'The old Slip.' Cyrus lowered his voice. 'No one's supposed to use the old slipways. They're abandoned. Well, not abandoned; they're banned.'

'Why?' Hedy whispered.

Cyrus shrugged. 'Don't know. But those bricks in the cavern wall? They're blocking an old Slip entrance.'

*Blocked in*, Hedy thought. The map tattoos wrenched in her skin, unsettled. *Does that mean I've got these for ever?*

Jelly leant in. 'How do you know all this?'

'My parents died not long after I was born, and I was brought up by the Sleight. I hear things.'

An orphan. Hedy had no idea what to say. She couldn't imagine life without her parents.

'I know this place better than almost anyone except old Brock Rabble,' Cyrus continued, pretending not to notice the girls' sympathetic looks. 'He used to be a Slip engineer before they were closed off. Flora says that's why Rabble's at such a loose end. Hasn't found anything better to occupy him.' He pointed ahead of them, where Ewan chatted animatedly with Grandpa John and Mrs Pal. 'He's not your average guard, is he?'

'You mean Ewan?' Jelly looked shocked. 'I thought he was hanging out with us because he thinks Uncle John is like some rock star from ages ago.'

'He does. But he's still a member of the Sleight. I bet he's really here to convince your grandad to give control of the map to them.'

Hedy scowled. 'It's not theirs!'

'I bet Ewan gave you that hair clip,' said Cyrus. 'The one that Jelly put in Max's hair.'

'No.'

'Huh. Are you sure?' He seemed deflated. 'Because it's a listening device. I was sure he was trying to spy on you. All the kids were using them two or so years ago.'

Hedy balked. 'But that Beatrice girl gave it to me just before.'

'Well, either she's stalking you 'cos she thinks you're interesting, or she's working for the Sleight too. You'd better flush it later.' Cyrus slowed his pace to let the others – Max in particular – draw further ahead before he spoke again. 'I know how to get to the old Slip. The way the map is telling you to go.'

Hedy stopped in her tracks. The idea that she might be able to follow the tug of the map tattoos, give in to their pull . . . it made her physically sway.

'We can't go on our own!' Jelly said. 'We don't know anything about where we'll end up. Uncle John would absolutely blow his top.'

'I can go with you,' said Cyrus. 'The Slip shrinks distances, right? I bet it wouldn't be as far as travelling overground. And he wouldn't blow his top if you brought Verdandi's Loom back for him.'

Jelly pulled a face. 'Oh, yes, he would.'

'But he'd forgive us,' said Hedy. She could almost see it now, their emotional reunion as she victoriously handed this mysterious Verdandi's Loom to Grandpa John. Just like she'd found the key to freeing Grandma Rose. Surely Candice and the Sleight would be impressed by such a feat if they eventually found out.

'Wait a minute.' Cyrus suddenly darted away to a stall that had small coloured notebooks piled up for sale. Just as at the ice-cream shop, the stall-owner seemed to know him, and let herself be sweet-talked into giving Cyrus a small number of the notebooks for free.

'These are telejotters,' he explained when he rejoined the girls. 'You address a message in yours to another person who's got one, and the message will appear in theirs. Phones don't work down here – no signal underground – but these are good for a fair distance. You can leave a couple for your grandad and Mrs Pal. Might make them feel a bit better being able to contact you.'

'Contact us?'

'Once we're in the Slip.' Cyrus smiled. 'I swear, this will be loads more exciting than the tournament.'

Hedy and Jelly shared a look. Then they picked up the pace again, quietly planning.

# CHAPTER 11

## SOUTH

The Vaults Hotel, where many of the competitors and judges were staying, was a complex consisting of four buildings set around an expansive lawn. There was a building of brick, one of sandstone, another of marble, and the last was made of wood.

The hotel manager, however, was thrown by Grandpa John suddenly arriving with a bear and a stag as well as unexpected children, and wouldn't let them into the room. 'I have Mrs Pal and Mr Sang each booked into a marble room,' the man said, his moustache leaping about anxiously as he talked, 'but they won't fit all . . .' he paused, lamely waving a hand at the unusual group, '. . . these.'

Ewan leant on the counter. 'What about a wood room? Couldn't you get one of those to grow a bit bigger? These are my cousins you'd be doing a favour for. If you'd just nudge a wood room in the right direction, I'll let Candice know what an obliging fellow you are.'

The manager's resistance crumbled. 'Very well. Follow me.'

After showing Mrs Pal to her room, he led the rest of them to the corner suite at the top of the wood building. Inside, it looked like a cosy log cabin. At the farthest wall, the manager put his head to the wood and seemed to have a conversation with himself. Then he put his shoulder to the wall and gave a shove. With a groaning noise, the wall moved backwards so that, in a matter of seconds, the room was more than twice as large as it had been.

'I'd better leave you all to settle in,' Ewan said. He looked as though he wouldn't have minded being invited in for a cup of tea. Despite what Cyrus had told them, Hedy couldn't help feeling that their cousin simply wanted to spend more time with Grandpa

John. *But that doesn't mean he's not following Sleight orders*, she reminded herself.

Cyrus also said goodnight to them all, and then quietly added to Hedy and Jelly, 'I'll see you later. I mean, tomorrow. And remember to do something about that hair clip.' With a parting grin, he closed the door behind him.

Although everyone was tired, their minds were still whirling too much to sleep. Doug and Stan settled themselves on the living-room floor and the children tucked themselves around the animals with a late-night snack of apples and Cheddar cheese.

For a long while, they were entertained by the Woodspy which had flowed out of Jelly's clog and was having a grand time exploring their wooden hotel. At Hedy's whispered instruction, it 'lost' the hairclip that Beatrice had given her somewhere in the building, although it kept coming back with additional items it found around the place. Through a knot in the floor-board it lobbed a lipstick, earphones, a miniature pot of jam and two crayon stubs. Everyone cried out for the creature to stop its scavenging, however, when it turned up with a stranger's pair of underpants.

'Grandpa John,' said Hedy, her eyes growing heavy, 'why don't you want the Sleight to have Verdandi's Loom?'

He sipped his tea slowly, then said, 'I don't trust that they'll keep it safe. I think they'll get carried away with what it might be able to do and be tempted to use it, heedless of the consequences. That's what magicians are like. That's what *people* are like.'

'You're not.'

'I learnt the hard way with your grandmother, didn't I?'

'So you wouldn't use it if you had it?'

Grandpa John shook his head. 'I have nothing to prove to anyone. Finding your grandmother didn't make me less nervous about what harm magic could do.'

Spencer placed his apple core in front of Stan and said, 'But don't you even want to study it with Mrs Pal?'

'Mrs Pal I trust, yes,' said Grandpa John.

'Imagine the magician's show you could put on if you could pause time!' Spencer's eyes danced at the thought. 'Flora seems like she knows a lot too. It's too bad you can't figure it out together.'

'She's part of the Sleight,' said Grandpa John, 'and they have an agenda that they're keeping secret from me. That's just how they are.'

'Keeping secrets?' Doug laughed deep in his belly. 'You're the pot calling the kettle black!'

'Or what's that other saying?' teased Stan. 'People in glass houses shouldn't throw stones?'

*Secrets.* Hedy guiltily wondered if she and Jelly were doing the right thing. But watching Grandpa John rubbing his face, the wrinkles deeply etched, she felt she had never seen him look so tired.

'Let's try to get some sleep,' he said finally. 'In the morning, we'll see if we can get home.'

Soft harp music momentarily confused Hedy, and then she realized that she had fallen asleep in bed after all. She reached under her pillow and turned off the alarm on her phone, then paused to listen. Spencer and Max were breathing deeply and evenly in the bunk bed. She hopped out of bed just to make sure they were sound asleep, and drew the blanket that Spencer had cast off back over him so he didn't get cold. The lights were off in the main room and there was no sound from Grandpa John's bedroom. After Hedy had gently shaken Jelly awake, the two of them changed from their pyjamas into day clothes, picked up their backpacks and shoes and tiptoed to the front door of the apartment.

Although they opened the door without any creaking, it wouldn't close as they stepped on to the landing. Not with a bear's snout poking through it.

'What are you doing, cubs?' Doug growled softly.

'Nothing,' Hedy whispered.

'I don't believe you.'

'We're just meeting Cyrus for a little while,' said Jelly quietly.

'Can't be a *little* while. You've got your backpacks, and I can smell all the food you've sneaked into them. You're going somewhere.'

'Go with them, Doug.' It was Stan, his antlers rearing out of the dark behind the bear.

'That's what I'm doing, Stan!'

'No!' Hedy pleaded. 'Stay here and tell Grandpa John we'll be back as soon as we can.'

'You're following that map. I can smell it,' Doug said stubbornly. 'Either I come with you or we wake up the Master now.'

After a moment or two, Hedy nodded and held the

door open wider for Doug to follow them outside. Although she didn't give voice to it, she felt better to have the bear by her side. Perhaps, if they were lucky with the old Slip, they'd be back before everyone woke up anyway.

'Tell Spencer to look for the telejotter notebook at the end of his bed,' she told Stan.

'All right. Don't do anything dangerous,' Stan fretted.

'We're not the ones in danger,' Doug whispered. 'You're the one who'll have to explain things to the Master in the morning.'

Cyrus was waiting for them by the edge of the hotel lawn. To Hedy's surprise, he didn't need much persuading to have Doug along with them.

'Might be handy to have a bear protector,' he grinned. 'I haven't packed any bear food, though.'

'You said we wouldn't be gone too long,' said Hedy.

'Let's not waste time worrying about my fat reserves,' Doug said gruffly. 'Where are we going?'

It was midnight. Although there was no moon shining underground, the mysterious illumination of the Fantastikhana complex had dimmed to a moonlight shade. No one else was around as they hastened away from the hotel. When their tunnel opened out across an underground stream, Cyrus beckoned them off the path to the rocky bed along the water.

They picked their way carefully downstream, away from the main tunnels, moving by the light of the girls' phones. The further they went, the louder the burble of the stream grew.

'Are you sure this is the right way?' Doug asked Cyrus.

'I'm sure,' Cyrus replied. 'I've been this way before. I sort of got lost in the old Slip and Flora had to come and find me.'

'It's the right way,' Hedy told Doug, at the bear's uneasy huff. She waved at the map tattoos on her face. 'It feels right.' With every metre they walked, it was as if she felt the tension easing little by little in a very tight string. She was on guard for that horrid pain she had felt when they had tried to get out of the main cavern earlier, but to her great relief it didn't strike. The Sleight hadn't set a ward down here.

They passed through a couple of small rocky hollows – made by people, Hedy thought – and finally came to a dusty grotto. Its ceiling was a colourful mosaic that seemed to mock them, deep underground as they were, by depicting a blue sky, white clouds and the sun. There were two other tunnels leading out from the grotto. They looked old but solid, with their mosaic tiles proclaiming where they led: *South* and *North*.

'This is the one,' Hedy said, pointing to the dark mouth of the tunnel marked *South*. The pull of the map was so strong that she couldn't resist taking a couple of steps inside.

'Hold on.' Cyrus unshouldered his backpack. 'I couldn't remember if the way was lit or not. You can save your phone batteries and use these for light instead.'

He handed Hedy and Jelly each a light torch. The tubes of the torches were shaped with the impression of a hand, as though a potter had gripped soft clay. When they wrapped their fingers around the torch, over the hand impression, light bloomed in the glass bulb at the end.

'Touch torches,' Cyrus explained, lighting up his own. 'They only need someone to hold them to work.'

As they shone their torches around the grotto,

Hedy felt a tug in her skin, and when she held her hands out before her, she saw the map tattoos twisting about. She let out a little yelp as she felt the marks moving in her cheek too. It took a minute for them to settle, and when they had, there was a silvery symbol on the back of her right hand: Π.

'Puzzlewood,' said Jelly. As Jelly spoke the name, the Π mark seemed to twitch. 'That's the symbol that showed at the place that Rabble called Puzzlewood. The one with the trees and bridges.'

'Puzzlewood it is then. Are you ready?' Cyrus asked.

'It's not too late to turn back,' said Doug.

Hedy breathed deeply, heartened in that moment to have Jelly, Doug and Cyrus standing there with her in the shadowy grotto. 'Ready,' she said, and she shone her light into the black mouth of the Slip that led south.

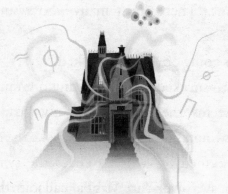

## CHAPTER 12

## MYSTIFY ME

'Why didn't you wake me?'

Spencer slowly opened the bedroom door and peered out. Grandpa John was pacing around as he admonished Stan, still in his pyjamas and with his hair in disarray.

'Where were they going?' he demanded.

'They didn't say,' said Stan, hanging his head. 'I don't think they knew, except that it was something about following the call of the map. Jelly mentioned meeting that boy, Cyrus.'

Grandpa John groaned.

'I did insist Douglas accompany them,' Stan pointed out. 'There aren't many who would like to take on a bear.'

'What's going on?' Spencer asked.

'The girls sneaked away in the night,' Grandpa John said. 'It seems they're following the map to find Verdandi's Loom.'

By the time Max woke up, Mrs Pal had joined them for breakfast.

'We should tell the Sleight,' said Mrs Pal. 'No one has any idea what the children will face.'

'But the pieces of Verdandi's Loom are just hidden, aren't they? They're not . . .' Grandpa John brandished his fork, looking for the right word.

'Booby-trapped?' offered Spencer.

'Yes. Booby-trapped.'

'That's the point, Mr Sang,' said Mrs Pal. 'No one knows.'

'What would the Sleight do anyway, if they knew? They don't have a map to follow the kids.' Grandpa John jabbed at his eggs. 'Maybe we should see if anyone at Pick Pocket Parlour knows a secret way out of here, then rent a car and drive to Puzzlewood. That was the first destination.'

'Unfortunately they might travel the Slip to Puzzle-wood a lot faster than we could by car.'

As the two grown-ups mulled over the predica-ment, Spencer and Max finished eating and excused themselves to join Stan, stripping leaves from a bushel of branches that had been left for him.

'I can't believe they left us behind,' said Spencer, irritably picking at a twig. 'I'm not a scared little kid any more.'

'Oh – I just remembered, there's supposed to be some sort of notebook at the end of your bed,' Stan said. 'Called a telejotter or something.'

There was indeed: a small notebook covered in navy-blue cloth, with a pen attached by a leather cord. Spencer must have knocked it off the bed in his sleep. Hedy had written his name inside on the first page. Turning to the next page, he found a message in her handwriting:

*Spence, we're OK. Tell Grandpa John not to freak out. I needed to follow the map. Jelly and Doug and Cyrus are with me. We'll come back as fast as we can. You can write me a message here in your telejotter. Start the message with my name, and what you write will show up in my telejotter. I'll let you know how we go.*

After a moment's thought, Spencer wrote, *Hedy, where are you now? Are you still OK? Why didn't you let me come with you?*

He couldn't think of what else to write; there was too much to say. He took the telejotter to Grandpa John and Mrs Pal, expecting the discovery would spark another anxious outburst, but in fact the two of them were relieved.

'At least we can communicate with them,' sighed Mrs Pal.

Grandpa John stared at the telejotter. 'So, do we cover their tracks and buy them time?'

There was a knock on the door before they could talk any further. It was Ewan with Chit and Chat.

'Good morning,' Ewan smiled. 'I thought I'd see if you wanted a guide this morning. Feel like heading out yet?'

'Er . . .' Grandpa John scratched his head, uncertain what to say.

Luckily, Mrs Pal called out, 'Hedy isn't feeling well and is still sleeping. But I think the boys are keen to explore if you wouldn't mind taking the rest of us around, Ewan? Jelly and Doug said they can keep

Hedy company here.'

Ewan agreed, and Spencer almost felt sorry for him. Mrs Pal just didn't seem like the sort of person who would fib.

'Could you give us twenty minutes to get ready?' Grandpa John said. He pointed at Max. 'We need to do something about his hair.'

'It'll be fixed when I'm 57,' said Max.

'That may be so, but right now I think you need a shave.'

The grown-ups let Spencer and Max take the lead, stopping at any stall that took their fancy. They gradually made their way around to a huge rainbow-striped tent bearing a sign saying *Mystify Me*. Balloons of all colours bobbed around it, without any strings holding them in place, and when Max jumped to grab the low ones, the balloons quickly shot upwards out of reach.

'Hiya!' called someone inside the tent. 'Come on in!'

A burly, bald man waved from behind a wooden table. His arms strained at his shirt sleeves, and his head seemed almost too small atop his hulking shoulders, but his smile was kindly. 'Whatcha got for me?'

'Um, I beg your pardon?' Spencer mumbled. He looked around the tent for some kind of sign to tell him what he was supposed to do.

'For the entry fee, you get to do a trick on me,' said the man. 'I get three guesses to tell you how I think you managed the trick. If I guess right on the first go, you walk out of here empty-handed. If I guess on the second go, you get to choose a prize.' He pointed to laden shelves around the tent. 'If I get it on the third go, you get to choose two prizes. And if I don't guess it at all, then *you*, my friend, can have three prizes, including one from the super-cool cabinet.' He looked over Spencer's shoulder. 'Oh, hey Ewan, how're them birds treating you?'

'Same as ever, Rob,' Ewan said, shaking the man's enormous hand. He seemed gratified by the way Rob's eyes popped wide when Chit, Chat and Stan came through the tent flap.

'You sure I can't buy them off you? Or how about the stag?'

Stan lifted his head haughtily. 'I, sir, am not for sale.'

'Good for you,' Rob laughed. 'Now, Ewan, what's the gossip? I heard a poltergeist somehow got into the

Fantastikhana and that's what pranked Candice's trick yesterday. Have the Sleight found it yet?'

As they chatted, Spencer and Max curiously inspected the shelves.

'Slime with hidden treasure inside,' Spencer read.

Max looked at the next prize along. 'Fox by blocks!'

'A thousand-and-one sound effects gadget!'

'I wish we had a trick that we could do,' Max said. 'Uncle John, could you do a trick to win us something?'

With a shake of the head, Grandpa John said, 'It would take more than an illusion to win down here, Max. And you know I don't like doing magic.'

Spencer racked his brain and suddenly had a thought. He unzipped his backpack. Inside was his spurtle, fat with the Woodspy in its middle. They hadn't wanted to leave the fickle creature roaming around the hotel by itself.

'OK, little one,' he whispered, 'I need your help.'

A short time later, Spencer and Max approached Rob, holding out the money for the entry fee. Rob's eyes lit up. 'Ah, someone's ready to mystify me!' He took Spencer's coins, then settled merrily behind his wooden table. There was a noise at the entrance to the tent. 'I'll be with you in a few minutes,' said Rob. 'Why don't you come in and enjoy a show?'

Spencer turned to see who his audience was, and found himself being scrutinized by Beatrice. Right behind her was Ned, looking more childlike and ready to be mystified than his daughter, although he hastily backed out when he saw Grandpa John and Mrs Pal inside.

When Beatrice smiled at him – somehow challenging and encouraging all at once – Spencer tried to squash his tiny flutter of stage fright. He faced Rob again, holding up the spurtle with its round, fat end.

'This,' Spencer said, 'is my wand.'

'It looks like a spurtle with a bad case of constipation,' Rob heckled.

'This is actually the most powerful wand you're going to see today,' Spencer continued, warming up. 'I'm going to enchant your table with it. I'll need your little hanky.'

'Pocket square, my friend,' Rob corrected him. 'This hasn't been anywhere near any nostrils.'

As Rob pulled his *pocket square* out, Spencer set the round end of the spurtle on the table, with his hand cupped over the Woodspy. He made some sweeping figure-eights across the table, and then whispered, 'Abracadabra!'

Rob snorted. 'The Lame Magicians' League called. They want their phony incantation back.'

To Spencer's surprise, Beatrice leant in close and whispered, 'He's trying to put you off your game. Don't let him.'

Spencer gave her a small nod, even more determined to win something. He felt the Woodspy drop out of the spurtle into the wood below, but he kept his hand cupped to hide it. 'Can you please hold your pocket square in your hand and place your hand on the table?' Rob did so, and Spencer continued: 'I have enchanted your table, and now your pocket square is going to disappear!'

The corner of the pocket square was yanked down into the wood. Not only that: a hole opened up around Rob's fist like quicksand and then closed over it, so that his hand was trapped in the table too.

'What the—?' Rob looked genuinely alarmed.

Spencer knocked on the tabletop again and, despite all his muscles, Rob's hand was shaken back and forth inside the wood as though a dog was on the other end worrying a stick. With another rap of Spencer's knuckles, more sharply this time, the enthusiastic Woodspy ceased its game.

'OK, OK,' Rob panted, 'this is good. *You're* good. Can you let me go now?'

Spencer banged the end of the spurtle on the table. The wood, however, stayed wrapped around Rob's hand, and the Woodspy didn't come to heel as Spencer had planned. He'd have to buy himself some time. 'First, you have to guess how I enchanted your table.'

'Fine.' Rob ran his free hand over his bald scalp. 'You made an offering to awaken the dryad of the tree that made this table.'

'Nope.' Spencer smiled sidelong at Max – they had at least one prize.

'All right. Second guess: a wood-based tweak to a law enforcement spell.'

'Sorry, but wrong again.'

Rob chewed his lip, stumped. 'Interesting, no one was able to mystify me enough for a third guess yesterday.' He thought for a while before clicking his fingers. 'The Lumberjack's Curse.'

Spencer shook his head, grinning.

'You won!' Max cheered, immediately dashing over to the shelves.

Rob bowed his head respectfully. 'Congratulations. Will you tell me how you did it?'

Something that Soumitra had once said came back to Spencer. 'A magician never reveals his secrets.'

'Fine,' Rob chuckled. 'But can you let me out now?'

Fortunately, the Woodspy understood that the game was done and won. At Spencer's strike of the spurtle, the wood around Rob's hand opened up, freeing him and his pocket square. A second later, Spencer could feel in his palm that the Woodspy had flowed back into the wooden rod.

After a lot of excited suggestions from Max, Spencer chose three prizes: a jar of slime with hidden treasure inside; a 500-piece puzzle that let you change the image once the puzzle was completed; and from the 'super-cool' cabinet, a pair of patches that claimed to be cheetah spots. Once pressed into the backs of shoes, they supposedly allowed the wearer to run as fast as a cheetah – until the spots faded.

'Cleverly won, young Spencer,' Stan said. 'I wonder how well those cheetah spots work.'

'Maybe I can race you when we get back home,' Spencer said, carefully packing his prizes into his bag. Then he stopped short. The navy-blue cover of the telejotter, which he'd tucked safely into his backpack, had turned cherry red. He pulled the telejotter out and opened it. The change in the cover's colour seemed to signal that there was a new message, because on the next fresh page, in Hedy's handwriting, he saw: *Spence, we've reached Puzzlewood.*

## CHAPTER 13

## PUZZLEWOOD

Hedy and the others started walking slowly at first, worried about what unknown things might pop out at them around the bends. When nothing appeared after half an hour, however, they began to relax.

Once they had left the grotto, the south slipway had turned into a tunnel that passed through rock of many types – light-grey rock, darker grey flecked with quartz, speckled reddish stone. Every now and then, the slipway connected with a natural fissure in the earth and they would find themselves walking through a humid, jagged cave. One of these caves narrowed to a cleft that rose straight up to a great height.

'I think that's daylight up there,' Jelly said, squinting upwards.

There did seem to be a tiny pinprick of light far above, but they all agreed it would have been near-impossible to ascend all that way to the top.

'How far do you think we've come?' Hedy asked Cyrus.

'Hard to tell,' said Cyrus. 'The distances aren't the same in the Slip. And Flora once told me they're not even the same from slipway to slipway. I've never been this far before.'

'The rock keeps changing,' Hedy said. 'Maybe that means we've travelled through lots of different areas by now.'

'Hope so,' said Doug. 'Our food and water won't last for ever. I like having a stomach again, but I wouldn't mind filling it up every now and then.'

'I saw a show on TV once where the people had to get water by licking rocks,' said Jelly.

Doug trained his snout towards a moist rock nearby and tentatively stuck out his tongue. 'I've had worse. Want to give it a try?'

'I'm not that desperate yet,' Jelly said. 'Cyrus, can you do any magic? Like, magic us water if we need it?'

'Nope.' Cyrus shouldered his bag higher and picked up the pace again to the slipway tunnel that continued ahead.

Hedy could sense Jelly smarting at his curt tone. Perhaps Cyrus did as well, because he added more gently over his shoulder, 'I used to be able to, but not any more.'

'Why not?' Hedy asked.

Cyrus didn't answer straight away. Finally, he said, 'Getting old, I guess.'

They walked for hours, and began to pass a few crossroads in the Slip. Murky tunnels branched off, teasingly – and incredibly – signposted as the routes to Belgium or France or Puerto Rico. Cyrus didn't know how long those journeys would take, and in any case Hedy's map tattoos never pulled her in those directions. As she headed the way the map tattoos wanted her to go, the undertow lessened degree by degree.

Not long after they'd had a breakfast of dried fruit and biscuits, the slipway walls began to change. Tree roots protruded down, the ground became earthy, and at last they came across the name they had been hoping for: Puzzlewood. Their way was blocked, however, by a great lattice of thick, gnarled roots.

Cyrus grimaced. 'Whoever bricked up the old slipway back at the Fantastikhana probably closed this off too.'

But the map tattoos in Hedy's hand tugged at her insistently. She placed her palm on the tree roots, but that didn't feel quite right – it was the silvery symbol on the back of her hand that wanted to touch the barrier. Hedy turned her hand over.

At that, the tree roots creaked and pulled back, opening the way to a slope leading upwards. Everyone gingerly stepped through and began scrabbling up the slope as the lattice of roots closed behind them.

'Wish I had your claws, Doug,' Hedy told the bear.

Doug let out a happy bearish snuffle. 'Can't describe how good it feels to use them, cub.'

It didn't take too long for light to appear. The moment Hedy saw real daylight, it dawned on her how long they had been underground. All of them began to haul themselves up eagerly.

Towards the top, Cyrus cautioned them to be quiet with a finger to his lips. They emerged warily from a hole in the ground, between the moss-covered roots of a beech tree. Hedy breathed in deeply, revelling in the smell of earth and leaves. Some of the tattoos danced restlessly in her skin.

Around them was woodland. Oak, ash, beech and other trees fought their way skywards between labyrinthine lumps of mossy rock. A frail ray of sunlight was doing its best to pierce the canopy of the wood. Close by, Hedy could hear small creatures darting here and there. Doug twitched as he spotted a dark tail slipping into the undergrowth; Hedy was sure that if he had been alone, he would have gone after it.

'We did it, we're here!' Jelly exulted.

Hedy pulled the telejotter from her backpack to tell Spencer that they'd reached Puzzlewood. She hadn't wanted to write anything until they'd had some sort of success to report.

'We're here, but what do we do?' said Doug. 'Hedy, where's the Loom?'

Closing her eyes, Hedy tried to filter out everything but the tug of the map. 'Down that way,' she said, pointing. 'Not far.'

She tied her stripy scarf to a tree branch near the Slip opening, so that they could find it again, and then they began edging down the slope. When they were halfway down, the trees thinned and they saw the bridges: spindly bridges of rope and wood, criss-crossing the forest over rocky gullies.

'Do we need to cross those?' Jelly asked quietly.

Cyrus crouched and aimed a finger at some rocks piled by a stream. 'He might know.'

'Who?'

'Can't you see that troll there?'

It was only when a lump of mossy stone moved that Hedy could see what Cyrus was pointing at. She and Jelly both dropped to the ground, trying not to be spotted.

'What do you mean *troll*?' Hedy asked, wide-eyed.

'An ugly magical dude who lives under a bridge,' grinned Cyrus. 'Classic troll.'

'I thought trolls only existed on the internet,' Jelly muttered. 'Are they dangerous?'

'Anyone can be dangerous,' said Cyrus.

'Then why would we want to talk to it?'

'I'll bet you any money that we need to get past it for Verdandi's Loom.'

Hedy looked up and down the stream. 'Should we circle around it and sneak past?'

But they were too late, for the troll raised his head, looked straight at them and waved.

'No sneaking now,' said Hedy. 'I guess we have to go and talk to him.'

The others all nodded and they reluctantly began to make their way towards the stream.

'Stay behind me,' Doug rumbled.

The troll's lumpen nose sat between saggy, wrinkled cheeks, and his face was framed by straggly hair that looked for all the world like brown lichen. His clothes were a patchy grey-green that blended in perfectly with the mossy rock around them. As they got closer, Hedy realized that he actually had moss growing on him. His only pleasant features were the small, dark eyes that studied them guardedly but without malice.

'Three mighty magicians and a great bear,' he said in a raspy voice. 'I'd call it an auspicious day.' Although she'd never seen a face like his before, Hedy thought she detected an ironic twist in his smile.

'Hello, sir,' Cyrus called out.

'*Sir*, is it? You're a polite one, aren't ye?' The troll gave a chuckle that made the single, enormous whisker on his chin joggle about. 'Here for Verdandi's frame?'

'Yes, sir,' said Hedy, following Cyrus's lead. 'We're

looking for Verdandi's Loom. Do you know where it is?'

'Look at the young magician with a fancy living map and all.' The troll gave Hedy a piercing look. 'Why are ye searching for it?'

Hedy hesitated, sensing that her answer had to be the right one. 'So that it isn't used for harm.'

'A good answer,' the troll grunted. He got to his feet, like rocks rolling about and standing on top of one another. 'I don't have it. I just guard the bridges. It's a family tradition, bridge-guarding. Come on, then.'

He beckoned them to follow him.

'This wasn't so hard, was it?' Jelly whispered, but Hedy had a feeling they couldn't count their chickens just yet.

As they walked, Doug said softly, 'Look over there.' The great bole of a nearby tree was teeming with rows and rows of familiar-looking round bumps, travelling under the surface of the wood.

'Um, sir?' Hedy said. 'Are those Woodspies in the tree?'

'They are,' the troll said.

'This is like being on a Woodspies safari,' Jelly murmured. 'This must be what they're like in the wild.'

'How d'ye know of them if ye've never been here before?' asked the troll.

'My grandfather has some in his house,' said Hedy.

'Lucky fellow,' the troll said. 'Nothing like Woodspies to keep everything in order, check on the health of the wood, keep the squirrels and birds from getting too rowdy.'

'You're joking,' scoffed Doug. 'The Woodspies at our house are agents of chaos rather than shepherds of orderliness.'

The troll whistled, impressed. 'You're the first bear I've ever met that lives in a house and has such a handsome way with words.'

'My room-mate fancies himself a poet,' said Doug with some embarrassment. 'He's a bad influence.'

The further they walked, the more nervous Hedy grew. 'Doug,' she whispered, 'do you think we can find our way back to the Slip entrance? I've been trying to memorize odd trees and rocks, but they're all starting to look the same.'

Doug sniffed the air and said, 'Don't worry. I can smell us back the way we came.'

The troll finally led them across a bridge of weathered wooden slats and rough shaggy rope handrails. Luckily, the drop of the hollow below the bridge was only a couple of metres. When a row of Woodspies headed past in the other direction, Hedy knelt to speak to them, but besides a very brief pause they ignored her, streaming around her feet towards the end of the bridge.

On the other side of the bridge was a clearing, and at its centre was a pale boulder. Hedy peeked at her hand – the tattoos were writhing in her skin, straining towards that boulder.

'Very well,' said the troll, clearing his throat a couple of times.

'*Turn this stone to book then flower,*
*Verdandi's frame is yours to keep.*
*But should you take more than one hour,*
*You'll find the scowles of Puzzlewood deep.*'

He leant close to the rickety bridge and whispered to it. Then he ran, with a heavy, lumbering gait, back across the weather-beaten bridge to the other side.

The earth of Puzzlewood began rearranging itself. Below the bridge, the hollow suddenly dropped away into a deep ravine, a hundred metres deep or more, completely surrounding their clearing. The ropes securing their bridge to the anchoring posts unravelled and the bridge dropped away, swinging into the gorge that widened with every passing second. When the shuddering of the land around them stopped, they were stranded on a small island, encircled by an uncrossable canyon, and with no bridge back to the other side.

'Ye have one hour to solve the puzzle and return,' the troll boomed from the other side, now much further away than before.

'What happens if we don't get back in an hour?' Hedy asked.

The troll poked his head out over the ravine to look below. 'Ye get to find out how deep *that* is.'

## CHAPTER 14

## THE BLANKET FORT

Hedy's message in the telejotter put Grandpa John and the boys in hopeful spirits. Grandpa John hastily scribbled a jot asking Hedy to be careful, but there was no immediate reply, so he closed the jotter up and suggested they bide their time looking at more of the Fantastikhana.

Before they had walked far from the Mystify Me tent, Spencer felt a tap on his shoulder. It was Beatrice. 'Where's your sister?'

Spencer told her their cover story about Hedy being unwell and back at the hotel.

'That sucks,' said Beatrice disappointedly. 'Well, do you guys want to come and see my next challenge?'

The Curious Construction challenge was too big to take place on the main stage. Instead, the Sleight had designated a bigger, neighbouring cavern as the building zone.

Each competitor had one hour to create a building inside their boundary, using magic and whatever they could fit into a single bucket. Spencer was fascinated by the things the competitors used to form their creations. Their buckets had everything from seedlings and broken bricks to bubble wands. One competitor even had a pomegranate.

At the blow of a bagpipe, the challenge began. It was as noisy among the spectators as any sports match Spencer had ever played in. Family and friends shouted encouragement from the stadium-style seats all around, or from the high walkways that traversed the cave overhead. Some got carried away and panned other competitors, but marshals quickly made examples of them by fashioning what looked like upside-down fishbowls that puffed over the detractors' heads and completely silenced them.

'Oh, good, they're using hush heads,' Ewan said of the bowl-shaped devices. 'Can't stand those rabid side-line parents.' He turned as someone tapped him on the back. 'Erm, yes?'

'Sorry, but we can't see,' said the man behind.

'Ah, excuse me.' Ewan quickly pulled Chit and Chat down from his shoulders to his lap.

'Not your birds. We can't see because of this one's hair.' The man pointed at Max.

'Oh dear,' Grandpa John sighed. 'Max, why don't you and Spencer go and see what the view is like from those walkways up there?'

Stan joined the boys up on the walkway, as though keen to soak up decades' worth of missed experience in a matter of hours. 'What has Beatrice got in her bucket?' he asked.

Chit and Chat swooped from Stan's antlers to get a closer look at her handiwork. 'Pegs,' reported Chit when they returned.

'And blanket,' said Chat.

Spencer, Max and Stan drew to a stop above Beatrice. The cockatoos were right: while structures went up at an amazing rate all around her, Beatrice was using her magic skills to make from her few pegs and tatty blanket . . . more pegs and more blankets, which she attached to a folded-out rack.

'She's an odd duck, this girl,' mused Stan. 'I couldn't help overhearing Hedy asking the Woodspy to *deliberately* lose that hair ornament that Beatrice gave her. Hedy didn't trust it for some reason. And Ned seems awfully nervous around Mrs Pal.'

'*And* her construction looks kind of lame,' Max whispered, not wanting to have a hush head plonked on him.

Spencer, however, felt it had been kind of Beatrice to encourage him at the Mystify Me tent. As the others moved along, he lingered a moment longer, trying to think of something charitable to say about her construction.

Beatrice seemed totally engrossed in her work, pausing only to check the time on an old-fashioned pocket watch. Spencer frowned. For a fraction of a second, he was sure a sliver of blue light had winked over her. Thinking uncomfortably of the poltergeist everyone was talking about, he wondered if he should call out some sort of warning. But what would he say? It would be mortifying if he caused a scene for no reason.

Moments later, there was a hubbub on the floor as disaster started to befall some of the competitors. Half-created walls fell over, windows cracked, roofs caved in and plants spontaneously withered.

'Someone's cheating!' one boy cried.

'This has *never, ever* happened to me before!' insisted another girl.

The marshals hastily announced they were putting up precautionary wards around each building site, to ensure no one but the competitor could work within it. But the damage was done. A good third of the competitors complained that they'd never get their buildings fixed in time. Spencer noticed that most of the contenders struck by the bad luck were those whose buildings had looked the most promising early on. Perhaps he should have said something about the blue light he'd seen, but it was too late now.

When the hour was over, the judges walked amongst the building sites to assess all of the marvellous entries. They spoke to the ground-level marshals about the vague accusations of cheating. There was no actual evidence of interference, so the winner was announced based on the merits of each building as it stood, but

Spencer thought the applause sounded muted and dissatisfied.

The boys caught up with Beatrice as she returned to Ned, looking deeply dejected, with her shoulders hunched and hands buried deep in her pockets.

'I should have chosen another challenge,' she said.

Ned shook his head. 'You did great. You might not win them all, but you can win *overall*. Remember what Maureen said.'

Beatrice gave him a surly look.

'Go on, get the fortune out and read it,' Ned insisted.

'She's just a stupid machine, Dad.'

'Go on!'

Beatrice drew a slip of paper from her pocket, just like the one Max had received from Maureen. '*You can win the Fantastikhana with nobody's help*,' she read aloud.

'There you go,' Ned said, as though that settled everything. 'Believe in yourself.'

As Ned tried to coax Beatrice into a more optimistic mood, Spencer spotted the treasure hunter, Bess, lounging not far away. He wasn't looking at the Curious Constructions; he seemed to be watching Max, Stan and Spencer.

'We're going to look around at the buildings,' said Spencer uneasily, wanting to get away from the man. 'Do you want to come with us?'

Beatrice agreed – thanks to some enthusiastic prodding by Ned – and wandered with them, noting each rival entry's good points in an envious mumble. There was Rainbow Cottage, a small house that sat at the end of its own everlasting rainbow, with flowers of every colour growing from pots of golden soil. Next to it was the Terrarium Lodge, a building and garden inside a clear, closed bubble that could sustain a family for ten years.

The boys almost missed the Invisible Hideout because it was enchanted to direct one's attention elsewhere, and seemed to be an empty space – good for criminals, the judges had noted with some alarm. And after that, they climbed a rope ladder to check out the Tower in the Sky, which hovered five metres off the ground and which, its creator promised, could ascend to the clouds.

The winner was a neat block of apartments. They weren't fancy but they had grown into existence in mere minutes, out of a miniature made of toy bricks. The Creator's Statement explained that she wanted to solve housing problems for the needy.

Beatrice saved her own until last. *Blanket Fort* was all her Creator's Statement said. It was hard to feel inspired by it after all the remarkable structures they had just seen.

'You pegged it really neatly,' Spencer offered brightly, feeling like he had to say something encouraging.

'This isn't all of it,' Beatrice said as though he was dense. 'You have to go *inside*.'

She pointed to a threadbare towel draped at one end, and Spencer got down on his hands and knees to crawl through. Once past the towel, he looked up . . . and up, and up. To his amazement, he was inside a mansion. Ornately carved doors were behind him, above was a glinting chandelier, and ahead of him was a pair of elegant marble staircases swooping up to the next floor.

'I would have totally voted you the winner if I was a judge,' Spencer told Beatrice as she crawled through with Max on her heels.

'Maybe it would have impressed them more if I'd been able to put furniture in,' Bea said wistfully. 'But I didn't have the time or materials for it.'

'Can you take us round?' Max asked eagerly.

Besides bedrooms – one for Beatrice and one for Ned – the mansion, empty though it was, was designed for fun. There was a ballroom, an indoor skate park with slopes and rails and ramps, and a trampoline room. There was a library waiting to be filled with books, and a thickly carpeted room for movies and video game parties. There was even a room for magical experiments.

Spencer was hopeful that the enormous kitchen would have some food, but there was nothing except a jar of tiny sweets in the shape of magicians with top hats. As Beatrice showed them the two greenhouses off the kitchen (one had many ramps and platforms for her rabbit), she and Spencer made a game out of trying to hide sweets in Max's hair without him knowing.

'I'd much rather stay here than at the hotel, or any of the other Curious Constructions,' Spencer said.

Beatrice smiled guardedly. 'The winner got points for solving a problem in society. I only solved my own.'

'What do you mean?'

'I split my time between my mum's house and my dad's house. If the Sleight will let me, I'm going to keep this as *my* home base. That way my mum can stay with me when it's my week with her, and the same with Dad.'

'Why wouldn't the Sleight let you do that?' Spencer asked.

'They said that when the competition is over, the magic of the challenges will expire. *What happens underground stays underground.*'

'Does your mum do magic?'

Beatrice shook her head. 'No. It all comes from my dad's side. *His* grandfather figured out he could do magic when he was a kid. He accidentally sneezed so hard that his head came off, but he didn't die or anything, and he could reattach it by holding his head on his neck and swallowing really hard with one eye closed.'

She pulled a cardboard box out of a kitchen cupboard and began rummaging through it to show them photographs. 'Here's me and my mum. And this is my grandmother with my dad as a baby.' Something about the second picture nagged at Spencer; it looked familiar, but he couldn't put his finger on why. She lifted another picture from the box, of her shaking hands with an old man dressed in a plum-coloured suit.

'That's Mr Rabble!' Max exclaimed.

'He's my tutor,' Bea said, 'but he hasn't even been to see me perform yet.'

'He showed Uncle John the map that ended up on Hedy,' Max prattled on thoughtlessly, 'and now she and my sister Jelly have gone looking for this thing called Verdandi's Loom.'

Spencer glared at his cousin, aghast. Max had blurted out the very thing they were supposed to keep secret.

Beatrice looked utterly dismayed. 'She's *gone*? But I thought she was ill at the hotel. Where did they go?' When Spencer made an evasive noise, she said, 'Come on, you can trust me.'

Feeling a little hurt, Spencer said, 'Are you only letting us hang out with you because you want to hang out with my sister?'

'No, 'course not.'

They fell into an awkward silence until Spencer, keen to change the subject, said, 'Ewan said the best workshop at the Fantastikhana is called the Foundry. Have you been there?'

'You know, I *should* start practising for my next challenge,' said Beatrice, taking out her gold pocket watch to check the time.

At the sight of it, Spencer froze, feeling a prickle all over his skin.

Beatrice didn't notice and shoved the watch into her pocket again. 'But the Foundry would be way more fun. Do you want me to show you the way there? And maybe you guys can come back here tomorrow after my last challenge is done?'

'Yes!' Max enthused.

Spencer didn't answer. Somehow, he managed to follow Beatrice out of the blanket fort and back to Grandpa John and the others without falling flat on his face. 'Are you all right?' Mrs Pal asked him shrewdly. 'Did Beatrice have a Ghost Room in her blanket fort? You certainly look like you've seen one.'

*I may as well have seen a ghost*, Spencer thought. The gold pocket watch. The familiar photograph of baby Ned and his mother. Her fortune: *You can win the Fantastikhana with nobody's help.*

Realization cascaded over him like a bucket of icy water. He had seen a small version of that picture nearly two years ago, inside the very same gold pocket watch that had belonged to Albert Nobody. That meant that Ned was the son of Nobody. And *that* meant that Beatrice was Albert Nobody's granddaughter.

## CHAPTER 15

## WOOD PUZZLES

As Cyrus and Jelly gazed at the chasm that stranded them in the middle of Puzzlewood, Hedy repeated the troll's words in her head. *Turn this stone to book then flower, Verdandi's frame is yours to keep.* They had one hour. Actually, a few minutes less now, since they had wasted time gawking at the transformed Puzzlewood. Hedy set a timer on her phone.

'I guess this has to be the stone,' Doug said, flicking his ears at the pale boulder in the centre of their clearing.

Hedy knelt by Doug to study the boulder and felt a writhing in her skin. The map tattoo was more agitated than she had ever seen it, the black marks twisting feverishly around the Π symbol on her hand. She could feel a new pull now – the map wanted her to touch the rock. *They've brought us this far*, she thought, reaching out.

Black tattoo marks coursed from her hand down into the pale rock. The lines spread in a vein-like pattern and then, with a cracking noise, the boulder splintered and fell apart.

Amidst the wreckage was a book. It was as big as one of those centuries-old books one might find in a museum, with a lock on its cover like a secret diary, and had only three thick pages. The entire thing – the cover, the lock and the three pages – was made of wood.

'*Oh. Em. Gee.* We turn our back for, like, a second and you've already solved half the puzzle!' Jelly threw her arms around Hedy.

'The map did it, not me,' Hedy confessed. 'Now how do we turn it into a flower?'

She picked up the book, wondering if the tattoos would help them again, but the map marks lay very still in her skin and nothing happened as she ran her hand over the cover.

'We need more than the luck of having the map to figure out the next part,' said Cyrus. 'Let me try.'

He took the book from Hedy and inspected it from all sides, pressing and prodding with no discernible effect. Then, to their surprise, Cyrus whispered to it. When still nothing happened, he tried again, more loudly – he was singing to the book. But it remained stubbornly unchanged in his hands. 'I can *feel* the book wanting to be opened, but it's resisting my . . . it's just resisting,' he muttered in frustration. 'If only I'd got my hands on it a few years ago.'

'Let me try,' Doug huffed.

'You can't *bite* it open,' said Cyrus worriedly.

'Who said anything about biting?' Doug held up his white paw and waggled it. 'This claw was made to pick locks. My maker was slyer than a fox watching a hen house.'

Doug delicately held his claw to the lock on the front of the wooden book. There was a crackle in the air, Doug's fur puffed as though electrified, and a fizzle of light flashed down his claw into the lock. The book popped open.

Hedy, Jelly and Cyrus cheered as Doug sank to the ground, blowing his cheeks out. 'I forget how that takes it out of me,' he said, lowering his head to his paws in exhaustion.

They found that they could only see the first thick page of the book – the other two pages wouldn't detach from the back of the first one. On the open page, a tiny wooden figurine of a man stood at the edge of a circle made up of a mass of carved pathways. It was a maze, and at the centre was a tiny wooden top hat.

Jelly touched the top of the figurine with her finger, and slid him a couple of centimetres along. 'I bet we need to get him through the maze to the centre, to the top hat,' she said.

'I wonder if this whole book is a book of puzzles,' said Hedy.

'Makes sense. We're in Puzzlewood,' grunted Doug. 'That's magician humour for you.'

They settled down amongst the broken chunks of rock to solve the maze puzzle. It seemed impossible: all of the pathways towards the centre were blocked.

'What are we doing?' sighed Cyrus. 'Wouldn't a magician's puzzle need magic to be solved?'

'Neither of us know magic,' said Hedy. 'No gifts, according to my grandpa.'

'Is there anything you could try, Cyrus?' Jelly asked.

'It doesn't respond to my . . . type of magic.' Cyrus bit his lip. 'But maybe I can try something Candice and Morten taught me.' He touched the tip of his finger to the figurine's head and stared hard at the maze, his brow knitted in concentration. Finally, he released his finger. '*The way home lies before you. Take it*,' he commanded the figurine.

The little wooden man trembled very slightly and they all held their breath, willing him to slide along the track towards the centre of the maze. But then the quivering stopped.

'It didn't work.' Cyrus angrily pitched a bit of broken boulder out over the ravine.

'Why not?' Hedy asked.

'Their kind of magic just isn't me. Candice would never accept that.'

'So what do we do?' Jelly said.

Very quietly, Hedy held her finger to the figurine's head, just as Cyrus had done. She focused on the little man and on the top hat at the centre, then repeated Cyrus's words: 'The way home lies before you. Take it.'

A buried part of Hedy hoped there was an un-discovered well of gift in her, that would spring forth in their time of need and save the day. That was how it happened in superhero stories. She was the grand-daughter of the Amazing John Sang, after all; she had saved her missing grandmother; she had the magician's map.

But the figurine was motionless. It didn't even tremble. She was still giftless. She was still a bog.

Dispirited, Hedy gave up on the figurine and fiddled with the wooden hat at the centre of the maze, twisting it.

*Clack.*

'What was that?' said Jelly.

Hedy gave the figurine an experimental nudge. The path of the little wooden man had been unblocked. 'The top hat moves a panel *underneath* the maze,' Hedy explained. When the figurine reached another unseen barrier, she twisted the wooden hat again, and the track opened up for him to travel further along. 'It's like another maze below the top panel. The two work together.'

Cyrus stared at Hedy, perplexed. 'How did you get so lucky?'

They attacked the maze with renewed determination. Jelly used a marker from her bag to show the tracks they had tried already, so that they didn't waste time backtracking, and Cyrus seemed to have a good instinct for which carved pathway to try next.

By the time Hedy warned them they had only forty minutes left, they were just one centimetre away from the centre of the board. Twisting and sliding, they edged their little man closer, and then, with a final satisfying click, he was there.

To their astonishment, the inanimate wooden figurine bowed, and swept the top hat from the centre of the board on to his head. 'Congratulations,' he said in a high, piping voice. And then he dropped through the maze, as though through a trapdoor. The first page of the wooden puzzle book turned on its own to reveal the second page.

Behind them, a shuddering started up again. The four of them leapt to their feet and saw two columns of earth moving through the ravine, bearing between them a spindly rope bridge. The structure butted up against their island, like a pier over the deadly drop.

'I think if we solve this whole book, we'll have our bridge back to the other side,' said Hedy. 'And we've got thirty-five minutes left.'

The second page was a sliding tile puzzle. There was no clue as to what image they needed to make, apart from what they could see on the tiles. At least two of them had eyes – so it was a face – and as they pieced it together they saw that the face had the black lines of a living map on the cheek. But it wasn't until the forehead, an eye and an ear had been connected that Jelly gawked and said, 'Hedy, we're making your face!'

They all leant in close to study the partial face that they'd formed. Jelly was right: a likeness of Hedy was forming in the tile puzzle.

'Why *your* face?' Cyrus muttered.

Hedy couldn't help feeling slighted by his tone. 'Maybe it's because I have the map.'

Although it was unsettling to see her own face materializing in the puzzle, it made their work go faster. They completed the tile puzzle with just over fifteen minutes to go. As the final tile slipped into place, the picture of Hedy became animated and said, 'Congratulations,' in her voice. Hedy was unnerved, as though someone had stolen a little part of her.

All of the sliding tiles spun over to their blank sides and the second wooden page popped apart from the third. Once again, massive columns of earth stirred in the ravine, and another bridge joined the first, stretching out towards the other side.

'Nearly there,' Doug said.

The third and final page was open to them, and out of the cavity spilled a pile of three-dimensional puzzle pieces. 'I think it's a tree,' said Hedy, picking up a piece that looked like a branch.

They dived into putting it together. Gradually, a hint of the final form began to emerge – a tree with something at the bottom of it. By the time ten minutes had passed, they could tell the tree had a person seated at its base.

'I don't see how one person alone could do this,' said Jelly. 'Look, it needs all our hands—'

'—and paws—' added Doug.

'—yes, and paws to keep it in place.'

Cyrus made a face. 'Unless you have magic.'

'We're nearly done!' Hedy said tensely, eyeing the timer. They had five more pieces to sort, and three minutes left. She scrabbled between the remaining pieces, trying to block out Jelly and Cyrus's anxious focus on the bridge. One, two, three pieces done. Number four fitted into the base of the tree. And five was the hooded head of the robed figure that was weaving at the base of the tree trunk. She placed it on the top of the shoulders.

Hedy felt something ripple through her – a marvellous sense of rightness, like hitting a ball perfectly, or making a perfectly balanced landing after a jump or . . . completing a puzzle. The chunks of wood trembled, and then, with a sound like a sigh, they fused into a single carved chunk of wood.

There was a rumble behind them.

'The final bridge!' Jelly shouted.

'Grab the book and let's go!' said Cyrus.

But the book had other ideas. It sank into the earth, so that it looked like the tree carving was growing out of the soil. They all held their breath. But the silence was disturbed, first by the timer on Hedy's phone warning them that the hour was up, and then by a low reverberation in the ravine. Although they had just prompted the last bridge to move into place, their one hour was over and the columns of the first bridge were starting to move away.

'Grab the tree, we *have* to go,' Cyrus said. 'Come on!'

Hedy shook her head stubbornly. 'No! Where's the flower?'

Cyrus yanked at the tree carving, but as its new roots lifted from the earth, rocks in the ravine began to crack ominously.

'Stop!' yelled Hedy. 'You're making it worse!'

Cyrus backed away towards the first shivering bridge. 'Come *on*, we can't get stuck here.'

'One more minute,' Hedy shot back. 'I'm sure of it.'

Jelly shook Hedy's shoulder. 'It's not safe, Hedy.'

'Start walking,' Hedy said, pushing her away. 'I'll be behind you.'

Jelly gave her a desperate look, then stumbled reluctantly towards the loosening bridge.

'You go too, Doug.'

The bear ignored her. 'I think what you're waiting for is happening.'

Out of the top of the carved tree, a single green shoot was growing and unfurling. In a matter of seconds, the tip of the shoot turned into a large bud. The bud flowered, and when it opened there was a curious thing hanging within. *This is it*, Hedy thought. She pinched off the entire flower, shoved it in her waistband, then bolted for the bridge on Doug's heels. Jelly was about ten metres ahead of them. And beyond Jelly was Cyrus, vaulting across at an impossible height and speed. How was he doing that?

The bridge jostled as they began to cross its weathered wooden planks. Hedy tried not to think of the depths of the ravine, but it was hard to avoid seeing those dark rocks far, far below, through the boards beneath her feet. The bridge was beginning to move, and if they didn't hurry, they would be stranded again.

Hedy and Doug managed to get to the end of the first bridge, but a gap to the second bridge had appeared as the column of earth began to pull away. 'That's nothing!' Doug called. He jumped neatly across the gap on to the second bridge, and it bounced like mad as he landed. 'Even Stan could make that!' he assured Hedy.

'He's a deer!'

'He's a lame-footed clodhopper. Come on, cub!'

Hedy backed up a few paces and then sprang across the metre gap, keeping her eyes on Doug rather than the yawning crevasse below. She made it.

'Next one, quick,' she panted.

Heart thumping, Hedy forced herself to hurry, edging her shaking hand along the rough rope handrails. The same thing was happening with the third and final bridge, but this breach was wider than the last.

Doug turned. 'We can make it.' He broke into a bear sprint and leapt across the gap, landing heavily but safely. 'Get a good run-up, Hedy!'

With her arms pumping, Hedy dashed towards the edge of the column of earth and sprang with all her might.

*Oof!* She landed on her stomach at the edge of the third bridge, winding herself badly. Earth fell into the treacherous drop below as her feet scrabbled for a foothold. But like a mother bear, Doug took the scruff of her sweatshirt in his teeth and pulled her to safety.

On the bridge, Jelly waved at them in relief, but then stumbled. Her clog had got caught between two of the wooden planks.

*Snap.* The bridge dropped a metre as one of the ropy handrails unfastened itself. The girls cried out in alarm.

'It's collapsing! Hurry now,' Doug urged. 'Go ahead of me.'

Jelly desperately tried to yank her clog from between the planks, but panic made her clumsy.

'Leave the shoe!' said Hedy as she reached her cousin, and they lurched onwards.

Halfway across, everything happened at once: the *snap* they had been dreading; all the tension dissolving from the bridge; the planks dropping from beneath their feet towards the waiting chasm below.

A rope was flung out to them from the other side. 'Grab it!' yelled a voice.

Both Hedy and Jelly caught hold of the rope and with a mighty yank they were reeled in, on to firm ground on the other side.

'Doug!' Hedy slid to the edge on her stomach, fearing the worst. But there was Doug, hanging by his claws, on the side of the ravine. The troll swung his rope down like a lasso around Doug, and with impressive strength, hauled the bear up to safety. They lay on the ground, breathless and stunned.

'Thank goodness you had that rope ready,' Jelly said to the troll.

'It weren't a rope,' the troll said as he looped it over his hand. He pointed to his chin, which now had a large pockmark. 'It was me whisker.'

'Did you get it?' Cyrus asked, kneeling by Hedy.

Hedy pulled the now-crushed flower from her

pocket. Inside the crumpled petals was a small frame of silvery wood that matched the symbol on her hand: Π.

## CHAPTER 16

## THE FOUNDRY

Spencer followed Beatrice to the Foundry along with everyone else, doing his best to mask his unease. Did she know anything about her own grand-father, Albert Nobody? Did Ned? Beatrice's father had stayed behind at the blanket fort, and Spencer wondered whether his awkwardness around Mrs Pal had anything to do with this revelation. Although wouldn't it make more sense that Ned would act oddly around Grandpa John instead?

The Foundry looked like a cross between a kitchen, a laboratory and a library. Its benchtops were inset with gas burners and sinks, and scattered with a fascinating array of tools, parts and ingredients. Most of the children in here were tending something half-made in front of them, and no two projects were alike, so Spencer supposed that each child had chosen their own idea. Grown-ups in well-worn leather aprons flitted to and fro, helping with advice or materials.

'I wish I was young enough to experiment in here,' murmured Mrs Pal at Spencer's shoulder.

'You've got your own workshop at the Palisade, though,' Spencer said.

'True.' Mrs Pal pointed to tall rows of moveable shelves at the back. 'But they have many more materials in those drawers and shelves than I do.'

Spencer thought about mentioning what he had discovered about Beatrice, but he couldn't safely do that until she was gone. He sidled over to her and tried to smile casually. 'Um, thanks for bringing us here. I guess you have to go and practise now?'

To his dismay, Beatrice didn't get the hint at all. 'I can hang out for a while.'

One of the Foundry's staff waved their group inside and seated them at a round table. 'Welcome to the Foundry!' she said. 'My name's Pip. Are you guys going to have some fun being junior makers today?'

'Do you think I could make something that will stop this young man's hair growing so fast?' asked Grandpa John with a nod at Max.

Pip bit back a laugh. 'Grown-ups can look on, but this space is strictly for *young* makers to build and learn.' She turned to Max. 'Is that what you'd like to make?'

Max shook his head defiantly. 'I want to do something with these.' He shook a jar that he'd pulled from his bag.

'What are they?' Pip asked. 'Pebbles?'

'Gargoyle poop.'

Spencer unzipped his backpack and retrieved the glittery slime that he'd won at the Mystify Me tent. 'And I have an idea for this.'

Delighted, Pip fired questions at Spencer and Max, and began to write up a list of materials. While they chatted, a stranger came into the Foundry. Beatrice seemed to recognize the fellow and, thinking he was here for her, began to rise from her stool. But the stranger waved her back down and handed a note to Grandpa John.

Whatever the note said worried Grandpa John. He

showed it to Mrs Pal.

'Why don't you go,' said Mrs Pal, 'and I'll stay here with the boys. They've just got settled in.'

'Erm, going somewhere?' Ewan asked.

'Just a quick chat with a possible seller,' Grandpa John said. 'But I'll be back soon.'

Ewan was clearly flustered, torn between accompanying Grandpa John and staying at the Foundry with the rest of them. But Grandpa John took the matter out of his hands. 'I know my way just fine, thank you, Ewan. Probably best you stay here and make sure that Stan doesn't cause too much trouble.'

'Trouble?' said Stan, affronted. 'Me?'

'Is everything OK?' Spencer whispered to Mrs Pal as Grandpa John hurried out.

'Yes, don't fret.' Concern lingered in Mrs Pal's eyes, though. 'Look, Pip is here with some supplies to get you started. My goodness, is that shaved sugarwick?'

Mrs Pal was like a child in a sweet shop as Pip brought more and more powders, tinctures and instruments to their table. She clucked with great relish at the ground liquorice fern, gum blossoms, camellia dewdrops and all the other rare ingredients.

As the boys set to work – Max grinding things with

a pestle and mortar, and Spencer boiling a solution in a small copper saucepan – Pip brought over a toolbox. It contained what looked like half-filled balloons, and an appliance that resembled a slim hairdryer.

'Are these Elusives?' Mrs Pal asked, eyes wide.

'They are indeed,' said Pip. When Spencer asked what Elusives were, she explained, 'These are ingredients that you can't touch – emotions and actions, usually. They're a bit hard to capture unless you have the right gear. This box has *Finishing a Great Book* – depending on what you're doing, you could come up with sadness or happiness. *Tasting Chocolate for the First Time* – did you know that not everyone likes chocolate? Weird. *Waggle Dance of a Bee* – that's good for making things that give directions, like compasses and maps. Spencer, I think we should give your potion a whiff of *Border Collie Brought to Heel*, for obedience.'

She helped Spencer fit an orange balloon to the blower, and then aimed it at his solution. The balloon deflated very slowly as a thin stream of the Elusive shot out and swirled the liquid in his saucepan. For a fleeting moment, Spencer very strongly wanted to be told what to do. He also felt like panting with his tongue out.

'That ought to do it,' Pip said. 'Now, let that cool and then you'll need to add three or four drops to your slime. Max, that pepper mixture is looking nicely pulverized. We'll need some teardrops from you next. Can you make yourself cry?'

'I think I can, if I pull out a nose hair,' said Max.

As Pip and Max debated whether he should extract a nostril hair, poke his own eye or sniff a cut onion, Mrs Pal began to wander the Foundry to unobtrusively look at what the other children were making. At least, she tried to be unobtrusive, but it was hard with Stan by her side.

'Is Mrs Pal your mentor?' Beatrice asked Spencer.

'I hope she will be,' said Spencer. 'I'd like to invent stuff like her, and run a shop just like the Palisade. But Grandpa John isn't so keen on the idea.'

'Why not? *He's* a magician, isn't he?'

'He doesn't do magic, though.'

Beatrice looked dumbfounded. 'But *why*?'

'He thinks it's unsafe,' said Spencer. He didn't want to say anything about Grandma Rose's disappearance. Pulling on that thread of the tale risked the unravelling of everything, including Albert Nobody's vendetta against Grandpa John. Beatrice was now the last person Spencer wanted to know that – and that was assuming she didn't already. To change the subject, he asked, 'How long have you been doing magic?'

'A couple of years. I didn't think I'd qualify for the Fantastikhana this year. I mean, some of the kids here have been learning since they were six. But there were a few wildcard entries that the Sleight let in. I didn't even know they *had* a wildcard draw until my name was picked. I studied so hard after I heard, because if I'm a wildcard, I'm starting out way down the rankings, aren't I? I'm already not as good as everyone else. The winners get a Sleight member as a mentor, which would be so cool because Mr Rabble's pretty hopeless at teaching.' She gazed around the Foundry longingly, and then said, 'Have you heard from your sister?'

For a moment, Spencer had felt like Beatrice was really talking to him almost as a friend. But her question burst that bubble and now he was sure she was just trying to track Hedy. So he shook his head.

A short time later, Pip told him it was time to reveal his creation. 'What I've made,' said Spencer, 'is Orderable Slime.'

'Orderable?' Stan said dubiously. 'Perhaps *Commandable* Slime would be a more compelling name.'

'Fine, Commandable Slime.' Spencer pulled a sweet wrapper from his pocket and placed it on the bench-top. 'Slime, trap that wrapper!'

The dark slime oozed like a fast-moving, glittery slug towards the square of waxed paper and enveloped it. Once it had the wrapper inside, the slime quivered expectantly.

Spencer leant down. 'Slime, harden!'

A second later, the slime began congealing, until it was solidified in a glittery mass around the wrapper.

'Now you don't have proper slime any more,' Max groaned.

'Slime,' Spencer said, 'slime up and come back to this tub.'

To their delight, the hardened slime slackened until it was in its original blobby state, and obediently slithered into its tub, although it still jealously held on to the sweet wrapper.

Max's finishing touches didn't take too long. He used tongs to roll his pellets in his powder mixture, and then Pip held up the Elusive blower for him.

'This Elusive is called *Archer's Triumph*,' she said. 'I think it'll help with aim. And this one is *Birthday Cake Sparkler*.'

She instructed Max to put the blower on low and blow two small bursts of each balloon on to his pellets. But when the *Birthday Cake Sparkler* balloon was attached, Max turned it all the way up to the highest setting and emptied the entire thing. Blanching, Pip switched the blower off. 'Oh dear. I hope it doesn't send them overboard.'

'Can I try it here?' Max asked.

Pip led them to a protected bay, its walls and floor scarred with smudges of past experiments. Shielding his eyes with a pair of glasses, Max lightly tossed one of his pellets towards a target on the far wall. He got it right in the bullseye and it exploded with a bright lick of flame.

'I think that was too much sparkler!' muttered Pip.

But Max shook his head. 'It's just right.'

He proudly let Spencer and Beatrice try out the pellets too, each one bursting with sparks and flame against the painted bullseye. Even Mrs Pal and Ewan took turns.

Feeling a mite jealous of the stir that Max had caused, Spencer returned to his slime and noticed that the telejotter in his bag had turned cherry red once more. Inside was a long two-page jot from Hedy, starting with large underlined letters declaring: *Spence, we got the first piece of Verdandi's Loom!* He scanned it all quickly, heart racing as he read about the troll and the puzzle book and the collapsing bridges. Seeing Hedy's handwriting suddenly made Spencer miss his sister. He wished she was here so he could tell her about Beatrice, but from the sound of things, Hedy was dealing with something much more dangerous than an unexpected family tree.

'She got the first piece of Verdandi's Loom?'

Spencer jumped. It was Beatrice. He had been so lost in thought that he hadn't heard her behind him, and she'd obviously spotted Hedy's jubilant headline. Snapping the telejotter shut, he shrugged and stuffed the notebook back in his backpack.

His secrecy wasn't lost on Beatrice. Her smile disappeared and the wary set to her mouth returned. 'I'd better get back to practising.'

'Well, thanks for showing us here,' said Spencer. 'Maybe we'll see you later?'

'Maybe. Bye.' She turned on her heels and left.

It was as though he'd actually offended her, Spencer thought, so did that mean she really did want to be friends?

Feeling bad, he decided a few seconds later to trail her to the door. She was already out and stomping along the edge of the main cavern. Almost absently, she withdrew the gold pocket watch from her jeans and turned it over in her hand, as though it was a good-luck charm.

Spencer's mouth turned to ash. For a split second, he saw a ghostlike form anchored to the watch. Blue-tinged, and hazy, it was nevertheless unmistakable to him: Albert Nobody.

## CHAPTER 17

## ONWARDS OR BACK

Hedy sank down on to the earth, not caring that she was muddying herself. After the terrifying race across the bridges, she felt horribly light-headed and there was a buzzing in her ears.

Cyrus gently plucked the silvery frame of wood from her hand for a closer look. It was about as long and wide as a matchbox, with two longer sides joined by one shorter stick. The wood had the slightly knobbly look of twigs and it seemed to have been grown into that shape, rather than fastened with glue.

'Want me to keep it safe?' Cyrus asked.

Hedy forced herself up from the ground, steadier now. 'I'd better carry it.' She carefully wrapped the frame and its flower in her spare sweater and stowed it in her backpack. Spying the telejotter, she realized she had better send Spencer a note about their first victory.

Her hands were barely steady enough to write. Why couldn't she bounce back as fast as Jelly? Her cousin seemed far from stunned, although she was staring morosely at her unshod foot, saying, 'What am I going to do with only one shoe?'

The troll lumbered to the bridge post and murmured something to it. 'If ye make them Woodspies an offering, they might bring it back,' he told her.

Jelly searched her backpack for something small that she could part with, and decided on a colourful badge with a small flag attached. She held it to the wood of the bridge, and soon enough a curious cluster of Woodspies sucked the badge out of sight. Moments later, her clog was ejected from the bridge on to the ground.

'Thank you!' She gave the clog a vigorous shake. 'Just making sure no one's hiding in here like last time.'

'Will the ravine stay like that, or will it go back to how it was?' Doug asked the troll.

He shrugged his bulky shoulders. 'No one's ever done what ye just done. This is all new to me.'

'What will you do now?'

'Oh, I'll be assigned to some other bridge. More bridges in the world than there are trolls, truth be told. And what will *you* lot do now that ye've got yer first piece?'

'I think we should take it back to John and Mrs Pal,' growled Doug.

'What are you talking about?' Cyrus cried. 'We've got the first piece! Now we go for the others. I told you it would be more exciting than the Fantastikhana!'

'*Exciting*? We almost fell from those bridges like flaming lemmings!' Doug exclaimed.

Hedy closed her eyes, experiencing it all again: the bridge slackening under her feet, the feeling of falling right before the troll had saved them. 'Maybe Doug's right,' she said. 'Maybe we should go back.'

Cyrus gaped, incredulous.

'It's way more dangerous than I thought it would be,' she continued. 'And *you* left us out there, Cyrus. You ran off when things started to fall apart.'

He looked at her, shamefaced. 'I'm sorry. Really. I panicked.'

'Hedy, you told us to start running,' Jelly said defensively.

But a dam had burst inside Hedy. 'We don't know where we're going. We don't know how long it will take. We don't know how many more ravines we might have to cross, or how many other bridges we might fall off. I haven't been so scared since...'

'Since what?' Cyrus asked.

'Since I had to save my grandfather.'

The troll leant in, intrigued. 'Save him how?'

Hedy shook her head, too tired to know where to start. So Jelly, with some help from Doug, told Cyrus and the troll about Hedy's adventure nearly two years ago, with its terrifying flight from a giant magpie Therie that had been taken over by the spirit of Albert Nobody.

Cyrus whistled when she finished. 'That's epic. You really did all that?'

'Maybe you're one of those born adventurer types,' the troll said. 'A Bess.'

Hedy frowned, not in the mood to be flattered. *A Bess?* She couldn't imagine that formidable man in black feeling as unsettled in the stomach as she did now. She turned her arm over and tugged her sleeve up as far as it would go. 'Look. The map marks that broke that boulder are gone.' On her hand, the silvery Π had been replaced by the φ symbol.

'The pull of the map,' said Cyrus, 'is it still there?'

Hedy nodded.

'Is it any less strong than before?'

'No,' she admitted.

'If we head back now, are you going to be able to resist that pull? Maybe Rabble was right. If you find what you're seeking, maybe you'll get rid of them all.'

Hedy rubbed the φ mark, reluctant to concede that Cyrus had a point.

'I . . . I get that you're afraid,' he said. 'That's only smart. But if we can find one, don't you think we stand a chance of getting them all? Now is the time to push on.'

'What's the big rush?' said Doug. 'Why can't we go back and reconvene with the Master, now that we know what we're up against? We need reinforcements. We need time to prepare.'

'We don't have time for that!' Cyrus nearly shouted.

For a moment, the whole wood was hushed by his outburst.

'What do you mean?' Hedy asked.

Cyrus dug around in his pocket and pulled out a few slips of paper. Hedy recognized them – they were from Maureen, the fortune-teller machine. 'They all say the same thing,' said Cyrus, passing them around.

Hedy found it strange that someone's fate could be spelt out in such matter-of-fact typeface. *Your gift resides in your mother's land*, it read. 'What does it mean?'

Cyrus took a deep breath. Finally, he said, 'My father was human. My mother wasn't. She was of the People of the Mound, the Aos Sí.'

'What's the Aos Sí?'

'Different kind of people. Not really of here. Sometimes they're called faerie. So . . . I'm half-fae, or I was. But when I was seven, both my mother and father died, in a great battle, defeating one of the Aos Sí who was making war on her people and my father's – your people.'

Silence fell over the group. Hedy swallowed hard, her eyes filling with tears.

'Well,' Cyrus continued, 'the tribe decided they wouldn't care for me any more, and gave me back to this world.'

'You're from a whole different *world*?' Jelly whispered.

'Not a world. More . . . of a *dimension*. Their world and this one are like different layers of an onion, they overlap but they're separate, see? The Aos Sí live in a different layer to us. Sometimes it's possible to travel between them, but most of the crossing points are closed now. Anyway, the tribe handed me over to the only human they had any contact with – a magician in Ireland. They told him I'd lose the part of me that was like my mother, the fae part. It would fade as I got older, and the longer I stayed in the human world. He passed me along to the Sleight. I've been raised by committee ever since.'

'Is that why everyone knows you?' Jelly asked. 'Because of your heritage? When you came onstage at the opening ceremony, everyone went berserk gossiping.'

'I guess so,' said Cyrus. 'Anyway, I think if I return to the lands of my mother, the lands of the Aos Sí, my fae abilities will be restored. I'll be what I was meant to be. One of those times when I can cross from this world to their lands is coming up, and it only comes around once in a decade.'

The troll tutted knowingly. '*Sow-win*. A time when the boundaries are thinnest.'

The girls and Doug had no idea what the troll was talking about. Cyrus spelt the word out for them. '*Samhain* – it's a Gaelic word. But it lasts a split second, and I need more than that to cross over. If I can use Verdandi's Loom, though, I can do it – pause time to keep the crossing open long enough for me to go back.'

'You want to *use* it?' Hedy frowned. 'But that wasn't the plan.'

'I know, but—'

'Is that the only reason you offered to help? Because you want to use the Loom?'

'No, I did want to help!' He turned to Jelly. 'I like you guys.'

Hedy rolled her eyes at this obvious ploy to get Jelly on side. 'But did you know you wanted to do this before we even started out?'

Cyrus hung his head guiltily, which was answer enough. 'I only need it once,' he said, 'just to borrow it for one second. And then it's yours or your grandfather's. For all it'll matter to me, you can give it to Doug here.'

'You aren't going to hand it over to Candice, are you?' Jelly asked.

'Why would I do that?'

'She's practically your mother.'

Cyrus scoffed. 'No, she's not. More like she's my boss for a job I don't want.'

'What do you think, Doug?' Hedy asked the bear. 'Is he lying?'

'I'm no liar bird, Hedy.'

'Can't you smell fibbing or something with your amazing sense of bear smell?'

Doug snorted. 'Besides Stan's self-puffery, animals don't lie to each other. Only people do that. I don't think my nose can help you here.'

'I believe him,' Jelly said.

After a searching look at Cyrus, Hedy at last said, 'Let me think about it.'

They shouldered their backpacks to make their way back to the Slip. Doug led the way, picking out the path by scent, and they were also seen off by the Woodspies travelling along their own highway of long tree roots and fallen boughs – discernible by the small flag of the badge that Jelly had given them.

'I'd always heard that trolls were a trifle mean,' said Doug as he plodded along. 'Bullying people and gobbling goats and such. But you've been more than fair to us.'

'It's a sorry reputation us trolls are saddled with,' said the troll. 'Folks spread vicious rumours, I suppose because they're jealous of our good looks. Although, I can't say no to a bit of goat, I'll admit.'

Hedy was slightly alarmed by the wistful look on the troll's face as he contemplated goats, but Doug was right; it had been heroic of the troll to save them from the breaking bridge.

She withdrew a few small packets from her back-pack – small ginger biscuits, trail mix and some cheese-flavoured crackers – and held them out to the troll. 'It's not much, but thank you for all your help.'

The troll's smile was like the sun rising over a rocky crag. 'A gift! That's powerful kind of ye, and unusual for magicians. My thanks.'

Hedy's stripy scarf was still tied to the tree bough by the slipway entrance. As they reached it, the troll held out the coiled length of his whisker to Hedy. 'Here, ye can keep it. Might come in handy,' he said. 'I'm not sad that you lot got what ye came for.'

With Jelly stifling a gagging noise beside her, Hedy gritted her teeth and took the whisker, trying to think of it as just a rope and not something that had been growing out of someone's chin. 'Thank you very much.'

'Good luck,' the troll said. With a final nod, he trudged down the slope back to the bridges that may or may not have had a purpose any more.

They clambered back down through the hole, then down the slope into the Slip. In the cool underground air, Hedy hung her scarf around her neck. It had been Mum's originally, but it was hers now. She wondered if Cyrus had anything of his mother's.

'Cyrus,' Hedy said, 'do you promise to give it back to us the moment you're done with it?'

Cyrus nodded gratefully. 'I promise.'

## CHAPTER 18

## LITTLE-KNOWN THINGS

When Grandpa John returned to the Foundry, Spencer was still stunned by having seen the pale-blue form of Albert Nobody anchored to Beatrice's pocket watch. But his grandfather had only one problem on his mind. 'They know Hedy has gone.'

Ewan looked genuinely startled. 'Gone where?'

'Into the Slip to find the Loom.' Grandpa John's eyes narrowed. 'What have they got planned, Ewan?'

'But you said she was ill and staying at the hotel,' Ewan said, crestfallen.

'What have the Sleight got planned?'

'I don't know, John! You seem to know a great deal more than I do.'

Spencer felt just a little sorry for his distant cousin, who seemed to be out of the loop on all sides, and would probably be upbraided by Candice for not having discovered Hedy's escape and reported it earlier. Since the secret was out anyway, he pulled the telejotter from his backpack and opened it to Hedy's latest message. 'They got the first piece.'

Astonished, Grandpa John and Mrs Pal pored over the message.

'This is incredible,' said Mrs Pal. 'A troll!'

'A troll? Can I see?' Max cried, hopping up and down. 'Did they kill him?'

'Stars above, is everyone safe?' Stan asked, accidentally-on-purpose poking Ewan with an antler as he nudged closer. 'Was Doug involved? Max, read the account out aloud to me.'

'Calm down, Stanley. No one killed anyone, that's just Max being bloodthirsty,' said Grandpa John.

'John,' said Ewan, 'if Hedy and Jelly have found the first piece, I'll need to tell the others. Now. I can't keep this from them.'

To Ewan's surprise, Grandpa John nodded. 'Fine.

We're coming with you. Because I want to know what they're planning.'

Sitting at the great table of the Peacock Chamber, Grandpa John told Candice – quite truthfully – that he didn't know how Hedy and the others had got into the Slip. He refused to explain how he had found out that the Sleight knew of Hedy's escape, although from the way Beatrice had known the messenger, Spencer suspected the fellow had been sent by Rabble. But he couldn't stop Ewan revealing that Hedy and the others had found the first piece of Verdandi's Loom. Spencer was forced to show them the telejotter.

'So, Cyrus is with them,' Morten said, with a side-long glance at Candice. 'He's after the Loom too. He'll want to use it.'

Candice rubbed her temples, troubled. 'Hopefully Bess will get to it first.'

'Bess? What do you mean?' asked Grandpa John.

'We've commissioned Bess to intercept them,' said Candice. 'The Loom is a dangerous thing, and must be kept safe. Weaving the threads of time is exceptionally powerful. Changing the past, directing the future . . . who wouldn't want to do that? Who doesn't have regrets? John, if you could get back all those lost decades with Rose, wouldn't you try?'

Grandpa John's eyes narrowed. 'Painful though those years were, I wouldn't undo them now. Such a change, so long ago, would change my daughter's fate. I wouldn't risk Spencer and Hedy for anything. Nor would Rose want me to.'

'Well, not all of us have your iron will, John. I will not let the Loom fall into the wrong hands.'

At that moment, Flora charged into the Peacock Chamber, laden with books. She was about to say something but when she saw Spencer and Grandpa John and the others, she stopped short. 'Oh, hello.'

Candice beckoned her in, resigned. 'They know that *we* know Hedy has gone. Does Bess have everything you've found out?'

'Every scrap.' Flora heaved the books on to the table. 'I learnt from these accounts where the other locations are,' she confessed to Grandpa John and Spencer. 'The second location is beneath the Isle of Skye, in Scotland. From there, they'll have to get to the Cave of Melody – that's Fingal's Cave. And after that, the Giant's Causeway, in Northern Ireland.'

*Isle of Skye. Cave of Melody. Giant's Causeway.* Spencer tried to hold on to these stirring names – he had to let Hedy know as much as he could find out. 'Are there trolls there too? Or giants?'

'No trolls that I could see,' said Flora, 'but a giant may well be part of it. And there'll be another challenge – the Kelpie King.'

Spencer edged closer to Flora's books, trying to read their titles. 'Kelpie King?'

'The ruler of the storm kelpies,' said Flora. 'Bad news for sailors. They sink those who don't play along with their game of "Finish the rhyming couplet".'

'But my sister is *hopeless* at swimming!' Max cried.

'Then it's a good thing Bess has already left, so that he can find them before the Kelpie King does,' Candice said with finality.

'Where is he?' Grandpa John said, pushing his chair back. 'I'm going too.'

Stan trotted to his side. 'And lest that foolhardy bear try to take on a giant – which I would not put past him – I'm going as well!'

'No,' said Candice coolly, 'you're not.'

'I'm Hedy's grandfather and Jelly's great-uncle!' Grandpa John shot back.

'Precisely. *Grandfather. Great-uncle.* You'll slow him down.'

'I held my own when Albert Nobody possessed a Therie to destroy me and my family!'

At that, Spencer knew he mustn't wait any longer to speak up about what he'd seen. 'Grandpa John, I think Albert Nobody is here.'

Every shocked face in the Peacock Chamber turned towards him.

'I think I saw him, sort of locked on to a pocket watch that Beatrice has. It's *Nobody's* pocket watch. She's his granddaughter, and I think he might be the poltergeist causing trouble all around the Fantastikhana.'

'Nobody?' Stan cried, his mighty antlers shaking to and fro. 'That spiteful spirit? That angry apparition? That ... oh!'

It was lucky that his grandfather didn't do magic, Spencer thought, because if Grandpa John had channelled the anger on his face, he would have blown a new tunnel clear out of the Peacock Chamber.

Prodded by the Sleight, Grandpa John recounted what Nobody had done at Hoarder Hill nearly two years ago: tricking Spencer and Hedy into thinking

Grandpa John had deliberately made Grandma Rose disappear; duping the children into releasing him from his chandelier prison to wreak havoc; possessing Uncle Peter to almost convince Grandpa John to burn his hoard of magical artefacts (this, more than anything, seemed to horrify the Sleight); and finally the near-fatal chase when Nobody had possessed a magpie Therie and tried to knock Hedy and Grandpa John out of the sky. The Sleight grew more and more discomfited as the tale went on.

Finally, Candice shared a look with Morten. 'Bucephalus,' was all she said to him, and without another word Morten strode out, his kilt swinging. 'Ewan, Flora, could you please go and collect Beatrice and her father Ned, and bring them here? I believe they have some explaining to do.'

After Ewan and Flora had gone, Candice said, 'John, Rani, if it is truly Albert Nobody, do you think you can help us contain him again – properly? And after that, I must talk to you about some more protective wards for the Fantastikhana. We're going to need them.'

Grandpa John looked at her suspiciously. 'You're just trying to keep an eye on us. You don't want our help.'

'As a matter of fact, we do,' said Candice.

'You don't want *me*.'

'Why wouldn't we?'

'Rusty as anything,' Grandpa John said.

Candice smirked. 'I don't believe it for a moment. Come, let me show you our supply room. The children and Stanley will be safe here.'

Grandpa John patted Spencer and Max on their backs and told them he would be back soon. With the Peacock Chamber suddenly empty of grown-ups, Spencer started rifling through the books and papers that Flora had left on the table.

'What are you doing?' Stan asked.

The thought of the stony-faced Bess tracking Hedy down stoked a defiant fire in Spencer's belly. He huddled close with Max and Stan and whispered, 'Let's find out whatever we can to help Hedy and Jelly and Doug get the second piece before Bess finds them.'

# CHAPTER 19

## SLIPSTREAM

Hedy led the way along the Slip, giving in to the relentless pull of the map. Her calves were aching and her right shoulder felt wrenched – probably from the yank of the whisker rope on the bridge. But she'd made the decision to continue, so she couldn't complain. Only Doug seemed disappointed by her decision to carry on their quest, judging by the displeased hang of his head.

A couple of hours after they had left Puzzlewood, the Slip began to grow narrow and more irregular, and the air began to feel more humid.

Doug stopped in his tracks, his ears twitching. 'What's that noise?'

They all listened. Neither Hedy nor Jelly could hear anything, but Cyrus said, 'Water?'

'I think you're right.' The bear sniffed the air of the slipway. 'Smells different, but I can't smell danger – danger that I know of, anyway. Still, you'd better let the Snowy Paw of Doom go first.'

With Doug in the lead, they pressed onwards. Soon enough both Hedy and Jelly picked up the sound of water gently lapping, a different sound to the trickle of underground streams they'd crossed on their way to Puzzlewood. Finally, the slipway started to slope downwards until it ended altogether. Ahead of them was water, reaching into the darkness. It filled the base of the slipway tunnel and there was no path to walk on at all. No ridge, no line of rocky outcrops; there were only sheer tunnel walls rising out of a narrow underground river.

'Damn,' muttered Cyrus, 'a slipstream. I wonder if we got lost.'

Hedy shook her head firmly. 'We're not lost. Not unless the map is. The pull of it is stronger than ever.'

'Down there into the water?'

Hedy closed her eyes to better focus on the sensation of the map. It was unmistakable. 'Yes.'

'How deep do you think it is?' asked Jelly.

They held their touch torches out over the water as far as they could. It looked deep.

'There's only one way to know,' said Doug and he waded down into the water. 'Water's nippy.' Three metres from the edge of the water, he started paddling. 'The tunnel floor drops away here, a steep drop. We can't walk it.'

'Are we supposed to swim it?' Jelly poked a tip of her finger into the water and let out a muffled squeak. 'Nippy? That's *cold*. Like, hypothermia cold. For humans anyway.'

Cyrus glowered at the water, vexed. 'We can't afford to lose time like this,' he muttered.

'If we can't swim it, we need a boat or a raft or something,' said Hedy. The water seemed to mock them with its gentle lapping.

'I brought my canoe,' Jelly joked, pointing to her clog. 'Remember Max said these looked like canoes? Seems like ages ago now. I wish Uncle John was here, he might be able to turn it into a real one.'

'*If* he actually did magic,' sighed Doug.

Unexpectedly, Cyrus beamed at Jelly. 'You're a genius.'

'Huh?' Even in the dim light of the touch torch, it was clear that Jelly was blushing.

'Do you remember at the Vaults Hotel, how the manager made your wooden room bigger?' Cyrus looked from face to face. 'I know that trick. Candice made me clean rooms there one summer, and I figured out how to make them smaller for a time, so I didn't have to clean as much. It's one trick I did learn how to do. Here, Jelly, give me your shoe.'

He laid Jelly's clog on the ground, just back from the edge of the water, knelt down and began to whisper to it.

'I hope he doesn't get any closer, Jelly,' Doug murmured. 'I can smell your shoe from here.'

Slowly, remarkably, Cyrus began to pull at the clog, wrenching it outwards, stretching the wood as though it was mouldable. First it was the size of a kitchen sink, then a bathtub. Cyrus hopped inside and began to push the clog (although it was hard to think of it as a shoe any more) even wider and longer, whispering to it all the while.

'Do you need help?' called Jelly.

'Yes, please,' he panted. 'Pull on that side. We need a boat that will fit us all.'

Strangely, the wood didn't feel soft, more persuadable, although persuading it to grow in the right direction required a lot of hearty pulling and shoving. Bit by bit, Jelly's clog kept expanding until it was roughly canoe-shaped. A few small branches popped out of the sides here and there; they snapped the branches off and Cyrus whispered to them as well, fashioning them into paddles.

The canoe wallowed heavily as Doug climbed into its middle.

'I could swim behind you instead,' the bear offered, looking worriedly at the waterline that threatened to creep up over the canoe's edge.

'It's not like you're *sinking* the canoe,' said Hedy. 'And we don't want to get separated.'

'Besides,' added Jelly, 'what if there are some sort of bitey creatures swimming around in there?'

They pushed off and, with clumsy paddle strokes, began to force the canoe along the slipstream. Hedy paddled at the bow, the exhausted Cyrus sitting behind her holding up the touch torch, then there was Doug, and finally Jelly at the stern. Having done some canoeing with the Guides, Hedy called out what advice she could to Jelly, but the watercraft swung erratically as they struggled to find the right paddling rhythm.

Trying to get more comfortable, Hedy grabbed the side of their vessel and suddenly the canoe jerked forwards in the water as though it had been picked up by a current.

'What was that?' said Cyrus.

When Hedy gripped her paddle to start working it in the water again, the boat slowed to its earlier sluggish drift. On a hunch, she seized the side of the canoe with her left hand again and, with that same little jerk, it began to slice through the water. The φ symbol on her hand throbbed a little.

After testing it one more time, she called over her shoulder, 'It's the map tattoos. They're pulling us along!'

'Brilliant,' Jelly cheered. 'My arms were about to fall off!'

They settled in to the ride, alert but glad of the respite from walking and paddling. After a while, Hedy glanced back at Cyrus. 'What can you do as a half-fae?'

'Hmmm.' He brought the touch torch closer to his face, pointed to his eyes and gritted his teeth in concentration. Very slowly, his irises changed colour from hazel to a dark purple. 'When I was ten, I could change my whole appearance. I could make myself look like you if I wanted to. Sometimes I'd change myself to look like Candice when she was right in the middle of telling me off.' He chuckled. 'That really used to annoy her.'

'What else?' Jelly asked.

'What else?' Gazing at the cold water slipping by, Cyrus softly began to sing a song. Hedy couldn't understand the words, but the melody left her feeling heavy with sorrow, pining for something she couldn't remember, something that she wanted to search for.

Abruptly, Cyrus stopped singing. His eyes returned to their normal hazel colour and the powerful yearning feeling vanished. 'When I was young, that song could have lured people to the Aos Sí's world. If there'd been a way open.'

Hedy caught sight of Jelly at the stern, gazing at Cyrus with a new spellbound intensity. Maybe the song worked more strongly on some people than others, Hedy thought, and she snapped her fingers at

Jelly to rouse her cousin from her starry-eyed state. 'That's kind of creepy.'

'I know,' said Cyrus, 'I never did anything like that. I'd sometimes use it to get people to give me cakes, or to get out of chores. Candice was big on me doing chores. I could curdle milk. Pretty pathetic power, unless you like yoghurt.' His expression turned wistful. 'The thing I miss most is, until I was about twelve, I could fly.'

'You mean you had wings?'

'No, no wings. Just could fly. Now, I can get a big bounce going and that's it.'

'So *that's* what you were doing on the bridges in Puzzlewood,' said Hedy.

Cyrus nodded.

'Why was Candice so cranky at you for wanting to be part of the Fantastikhana?' Jelly asked.

'The Sleight want me to wean myself off my fae gift. See, it's different magic to what Candice and everyone at the Fantastikhana do. Humans almost always need an object of some sort to channel and do magic. Wands or looms or shells or whatever else, to capture power and direct it. With the Aos Sí, the magic is raw, it flows out of you. But it's like a stream is drying up in me the older I get, the closer I get to my birthday. So, this year, I wanted one last hurrah at the Fantastikhana. Just to remind everyone who I am.' His expression turned bitter. 'Candice is always telling me, "Stop dwelling on the past and embrace your future."'

'Can you learn to do normal magic?' Hedy asked. 'I mean, could you do things like the other kids in the Fantastikhana? Non-fae magic?'

'You sound like Candice. It's not the same.'

'How is it different?'

Cyrus trailed his fingers in the slipstream. 'Imagine you could open your mouth to sing and the sound of a symphony orchestra poured out. And then imagine losing that and being told you could still make music – *if* you learn every single instrument in the orchestra. But you can't play them all at once, can you, so you'll never recreate that sound. *That's* how different it is.' The pain in his voice was palpable. 'That part of me is dwindling away to nothing, and soon I'll be as ordinary as anyone else. Unless I can get back to my mother's homeland.'

Lost in their own thoughts, they glided for a long time in silence, until the canoe began to judder, shrinking and growing fitfully.

'Cyrus, how long will your expand-a-shoe spell work for?' Jelly asked, looking alarmed.

Cyrus patted the canoe like it was a fretting animal. 'At the hotel, the wood just stayed put until it was ordered to change.'

The canoe quivered again. 'Why's it doing this?' Jelly yelped.

'I don't know. I've never made a boat before.'

Doug lifted his snout, peering keenly down the tunnel. 'What's up there?'

Pinpricks of light were glimmering in the wall of the slipstream ahead. Instinctively, Hedy took her hand from the canoe to slow them down, and they coasted slowly alongside words that shone out of the rock.

*Those who come to seek the Loom*
*Of fate are destined to their doom,*
*If glory is taken from the throne*
*And kindness drowns like Verdandi's stone.*

'Well, that's comforting,' rumbled Doug, when Hedy had read the verse aloud for him. 'What does it mean?'

'It reminds me of the troll's verse,' said Hedy. Not wanting to forget it, she rummaged for her phone to take a picture. 'Is it a sort of clue?'

'Pretty cryptic clue,' Jelly grumbled, 'and not very encouraging.'

The battery on her phone had run out, so Hedy pulled the telejotter out of her backpack to copy the verse in there. The cover had changed to red again; a message was waiting in Spencer's spiky handwriting.

*Hedy, the Sleight are sending Bess after you guys. He's going to take the Loom pieces for them, so that you don't use it. And Flora said the second location is the Isle of Skye, all the way up in Scotland. And you might have to beat some guy called the Kelpie King. He sinks sailors who don't do some rhyming verse challenge. And then the last place on the map is in Northern Ireland, the Giant's Causeway. I'll keep trying to find out more.*

'Damn!' said Cyrus. 'Not Bess!'

'How's he going to find us?' Jelly asked. 'He doesn't have a map like Hedy. And he's way behind us.'

'Besses are really skilled trackers and seekers,' said Cyrus. 'If he knows the area we're in, he won't need a map. I bet they're opening up an old slipway for him to find us. We have to find the pieces before he does.'

'What about this Kelpie King that Spencer wrote about?' said Doug. 'Have you ever heard of him?'

Hedy glanced up from the verse she'd been writing

in the telejotter. 'He must have something to do with the "throne" from the clue.'

Their chance to decipher anything more evaporated when the canoe suddenly shot down the slipstream so quickly that the air whistled in their ears. As it accelerated, Hedy gripped the side, white-knuckled, feeling sure that they would careen and smash into the rocky walls if she let go. An urge to shout was building up in her chest. Just when she thought she would have to let the scream out, their little watercraft was spat out into a lake that filled the bottom of a huge cave.

## CHAPTER 20

## DUEL

The roof of the cave was as high as a cathedral ceiling. Small pulsing globes hung up there, encircled by thick threads of sparkling crystal drops.

'A star-filled night in a quiet glade never looked so beautiful,' said Doug. 'I wish Stan could see this. He'd find words to do it justice.'

Hedy smiled. 'You just did pretty well yourself, Doug.'

Their canoe skimmed past one of the stone stalactites scattered across the lake. On a whim, Hedy put her hand on the stalactite to see if the tattoos would do something like they had with the boulder, but although they were swimming in her skin, they didn't leave her. Clasping the side of the canoe didn't propel it through the water any more.

'Anything, cub?' Doug asked her.

Hedy shook her head and took up a paddle. 'I can't tell which way they're pulling me. They just want to be . . . here.'

Towards the centre of the lake, the threads of crystals hung very low, and some of the strands inched downwards invitingly as they approached.

'Whoa, hang back,' Cyrus warned as their canoe glided closer.

At the bow, Hedy realized why Cyrus was worried. The threads weren't glistening with crystals; they were hung with huge wet drops of something clear and sticky. But their paddling was clumsy, and they couldn't stop their momentum fast enough to avoid swinging through a cluster of threads.

'Duck!' Cyrus cried.

Hedy, Jelly and Cyrus all bent low, but Doug, larger than any of them, didn't quite manage to get out of the way. The very tips of a few threads swiped the bear and stuck to him.

'Argh! Get 'em off me!' he yelled, slapping a paw at the threads to break free. But the sticky blobs – so pretty a moment ago – trapped his paw as well. The more Doug struggled, the more he was caught fast. And then the threads began to edge upwards, towards the pulsing globes on the ceiling of the cave, dragging Doug aloft.

*They're like massive glow-worms catching prey*, Hedy realized in horror.

Shouting wildly, they tried to pull at Doug without touching the gluey drops and getting trapped themselves. The canoe rocked dangerously from side to side, threatening to pitch them into the dark water. Doug thrashed and growled in the air, only to find that the more he flailed, the worse he was entangled and the higher he was reeled upwards.

As they frantically tried to free Doug, the water of the lake began to bubble and churn. They had no choice but to let go of Doug's dangling hind legs and crouch low in the canoe so that they didn't fall overboard.

'Oh em gee, there are people in there,' said Jelly, pointing at the bubbles.

Rising up through the water were figures the size and shape of humans, but their skin was a greyish blue.

'Are they Smurfs?' Jelly whispered hoarsely. 'Big, friendly water ones?'

As they swam about, they splashed the canoe and sang to each other with boisterous, musical voices, in a language that Hedy and Jelly couldn't make out. Cyrus, however, twisted and turned, trying to catch their words as though they hovered on the cusp of understanding.

'I think they're storm kelpies,' said Cyrus.

'What are storm kelpies?' said Hedy urgently.

'Sea spirits. They like to capsize boats.'

Hedy's stomach flipped over in fear. *Great.* At her feet, the fallen telejotter had turned red again; Spencer had written something to her: *Hedy, where are you now?*

The blue men let out a great whooping hullabaloo as something much larger began to rise from beneath the surface of the water. It was a throne of rough-cut dull crystal. Seated upon it, with water streaming from his head and body, was a blue man whose hair looked like lanky strands of seaweed. He wore a tall crown that looked like it had been fashioned from stalagmites, and had a piercing stare. At the thought of having to go up against him, Hedy suddenly regretted wanting to impress Candice Harding.

She wrote back to Spencer, *Looking at the Kelpie King.*

The king held up a hand to silence his rowdy companions. As their echoes dwindled, he spoke. 'Young sailors, you are far from home. What do you seek in the dark sea foam?'

Heart beating fast, Hedy stammered, 'We're here for Verdandi's Loom.'

The storm kelpies waited expectantly. But when Hedy said nothing else, they shrieked with laughter and dived all around the canoe, jostling the watercraft and drenching Hedy, Jelly and Cyrus.

The king smiled slyly as he spoke once more in the manner of someone reciting poetry.

*'The weighing stone is far from here, unless I judge you best*

*In rhyming couplets with the king. Trounce me to end your quest.'*

He pointed a blue finger at Doug hanging helplessly over the water and went on:

*'I see the glow-worms' silken threads have trapped your fearsome friend.*

*Defeat me in a poetry duel to save him from his end.'*

Jelly groaned into her hands. 'Is King Seaweed

challenging us to a ye olde rhyming rap battle?'

'Ah, of course! That's what Spencer meant,' Cyrus realized. 'It's what they're notorious for.'

'Are we going to accept?'

'We don't have a choice,' Hedy said. She called out to the king, 'All right, we're ready to start.'

Rubbing his hands together, the king stood from his throne and then declared,

*Verdandi's stone sits undersea,*
*How did you find this place?'*

'Write it down,' Jelly urged Hedy in a whisper, 'otherwise we'll forget what we have to rhyme with.'

Hedy hastily scribbled it down in the telejotter as Jelly and Cyrus muttered it over and over, thinking. But the stress of the situation made all three of them impatient, tetchy and unable to come up with anything.

*What's that?* Spencer wrote.

*Poetry challenge,* Hedy wrote back.

A minute later, Spencer shocked them with a line of verse, so that the whole thing read:

*Verdandi's stone sits undersea,*
*How did you find this place?*
*We used Old River water to see*

*The map by which we trace.*

They gaped.

*That was Stan, by the way*, added Spencer.

'Should I try it?' Hedy asked the others.

'It's better than anything we've come up with,' said Cyrus.

Hedy wobbled to her feet and read the words out aloud. The king scowled and nodded once, prompting the blue men around the canoe to dash their hands in the water, sour with disappointment. Evidently, Hedy had recited a verse that passed muster. *Thank you, Stan!* she wrote in the telejotter. *I think you've saved Doug from gluey giant glow-worm threads!*

But the king wasn't done yet. With a flamboyant clearing of the throat, he next called out:

'*Should you win this prize of yore,*
*What will your crew then do?*'

'What rhymes with yore?' Jelly mumbled, as Hedy scrawled the words in the telejotter. 'Score. Snore. Bore! And what rhymes with do? I know what Max would say rhymes with do . . .'

But again, before they could agree on a rejoinder, Spencer wrote a response.

*Away we'll voyage, to find one more,*

*And bid the king adieu.*

When Hedy read the words aloud, there was even an approving murmur amongst the storm kelpies.

'This sticky gunk is starting to harden!' Doug called out in a muffled voice. 'Having trouble moving!'

'Hang in there, we're going to do this,' Hedy reassured him. But when she turned back to the Kelpie King, a devious smirk played across his face that made her wonder if she'd just jinxed them.

The king said:

'*You must choose between your captured bear*
*And the Loom to leave this cave.*'

They all froze at his words.

Finally, Hedy burst out, 'That's not fair! You said if we defeated you, we'd save him.'

With an amused flick of his seaweed hair, the king told them:

'*Cry not, my words played no mean trick.*
*Defeat the king, then take your pick.*
*Tell me which, with your next rhyme,*
*or he'll hang like them for the rest of time.*'

As he said 'them', the king pointed to the rocky stalactite pillars scattered about the vast cave. That was when Hedy began to see that that pillar's jutting fragment seemed just like an arm encased in rock . . . and the bulge in that pillar looked exactly like it had a head within it . . . and protruding from that stalactite was a twitching foot.

'Do those stalactites have people trapped inside?' asked Hedy, gaping at the black-booted foot in horror. How could they have missed that before?

The king's smile grew even wider. Around them, the swimming storm kelpies began chanting, filling the cave with echoes of the king's challenge:

*You must choose between your captured bear*
*And the Loom to leave this cave . . .*

Hedy's hand felt leaden. She couldn't bring herself to write down the words in the telejotter. Jelly grabbed it from her, dashing off words and crossing them out.

'What are we going to do?' asked Cyrus.

'We . . .' Hedy paused, gathering her thoughts. 'We get Doug, and then we try to get in here again. Only *next* time we don't go anywhere near those glow-worm threads. That way we don't need to make a choice.'

'How do you know we can get back in here again?' Cyrus demanded.

'The tattoos will guide us. They did once, they can do it again.'

'And what about that poor sod whose boot we can see? Are you going to choose to save him too? Bess is coming after us, Hedy, and we're running out of time! The way to my mother's homeland is open for only the smallest sliver of a moment, once every ten years. If I miss this chance, it's too late.'

'We can't leave Doug here, Cyrus. He's not just a rug. It would be like leaving you or me or Jelly behind.'

Cyrus turned to Jelly. 'What do you think, Jelly?'

Jelly looked thoroughly miserable as she said to Cyrus, 'I'm sorry.'

And then she stood up shakily in the canoe and replied to the Kelpie King with the verse that she had quietly composed while Hedy and Cyrus had been arguing:

'*Though the Loom is precious and rare,*
*It's the living we choose to save.*'

With the last line, Jelly gestured at both Doug and the stalactite with the jerking boot. Hedy held her breath as all the blue men quietly murmured to each other. The king's eyes narrowed at Jelly and Hedy. Then he clapped slowly, three times, whipped his crown from his head and flung it, like a discus, towards Doug.

'No!' Hedy shouted, fearing the crown was going to strike her friend. But the spinning crown soared high, right through the sticky threads above the bear's head, cutting him free. Doug dropped like a rock into the lake below. The crown whirred out and around to the stalactite with the protruding boot and sliced through its top as well, sending the rocky formation – and whoever was inside it – crashing into the lake.

The storm kelpies dived beneath the water and, moments later, three of them dragged Doug to the surface, spluttering and growling, but washed free of the thick goo in which he had been trapped. Laughing raucously, the storm kelpies hoisted him back into the canoe as though a waterlogged bear weighed no more than a child. It took some time for other storm kelpies to emerge with the fallen stalactite, and they began striking it hard with rocks to chisel the prisoner free.

Upon his throne, the king toyed with the crown, which had whirled back to him, and said:

*'The choice was made, your friend is free.*
*You've shown rare kindness, we all agree.*
*If your hearts had been untrue,*
*The worms above would have trapped you too.'*

His eyes flicked to the water before him, which

rippled and then seethed. From the centre of that churning water ascended a huge bubble. The higher it rose, the more agitated the map tattoos in Hedy's skin became. Louder now, the king went on:

*'And so, the prize rises from the deep.*
*Should black lines wake it from its sleep,*
*Verdandi's weighing stone is yours to keep.'*

*Black lines.* Hedy knew what to do. She paddled the canoe forwards and reached out a shaky hand. As her fingers, her hand, and then her arm slipped through the bubble's surface, the map tattoos lifted off her skin and wound their way around the clear dome.

Inside, the tips of her fingers brushed against something, a ring-shaped stone. Hedy grabbed it and yanked her hand back, bursting the bubble. The tattoos were gone – how strangely light she felt without those now – but in her hand was the second piece of the Loom. It seemed to be made of quartz – one half of the circle a dark smoky colour, and the other clear. Set in the ring was a silvery symbol: $\phi$. The same symbol that had shone in her hand was now gone.

Hedy held it up to the others triumphantly. But she had no time to crow to Cyrus that they had made the best choice after all, because suddenly everything was happening at once. A whirlpool was starting to swirl where the bubble had been, and the storm kelpies were swimming away from it, filling the cave with a song:

*'Sing yellow, sing blue, sing red, sing green,*
*That's how the slipway shall be seen!*
*Jump yellow, jump blue, jump green, jump red,*
*Run where the giants feared to tread!'*

Most shockingly of all, Hedy could see that the now-freed prisoner, who was slowly sinking in the water, was dressed all in black. It was Bess.

'Oh, no! Hold on!' Cyrus yelled out to them all as the whirlpool twisted faster and faster, drawing their canoe in no matter how hard they paddled. And then, with a stomach-heaving wrench, and the song echoing in their ears, they were sucked into the heart of the vortex.

## CHAPTER 21

## TO UNDO THE UNBEARABLE DECISION

'Any word from them?' Stan asked for the twentieth time.

Spencer shook his head. When the danger to Doug had become clear with the final couplet, even Stan had been too appalled to think of an answering line of verse. They'd been heartened when Jelly's handwriting had appeared in the telejotter, but now the silence of the blank page left them in a suspense that had Stan pacing nervously and Spencer's stomach in a twist. He wondered if the raisin pastry on the sideboard would settle it.

'Surely he must be free by now,' Stan muttered. 'I doubt there's a thread in the world that could hold that shaggy bear lump for any decent period of time.'

They were still staring helplessly at the telejotter when Grandpa John, Mrs Pal and the Sleight returned to the Peacock Chamber. Beatrice and Ned were brought in by Flora, with a hunted look about them.

'A good thing you told Bucephalus to bar their exit,' Flora said. 'They somehow knew we had questions for them and were trying to slip out of the Fantastikhana.'

Candice studied both Beatrice and Ned frostily. 'You didn't catch the poltergeist and trap it, did you? You were in league with it, and sneaked it in pretending it was your captive, to get it past our wards. Is it true it's your father?'

Beatrice and Ned stared at their shoes for a long time as the silence steadily grew heavier and heavier. Finally, Beatrice looked up, ready to speak, but Ned suddenly tugged his hand from his pocket. He had a small, spotted feather in his palm.

'Dad, no!' Beatrice yelled.

But Ned, casting a sorry look at his daughter, blew the feather off his hand before she could stop him. Sensing that something dreadful was about to happen,

Spencer dragged Max backwards to hunker by the wall.

By the time the feather wafted to the ground, every single grown-up in the room, including Ned, had shrunk and transformed. Limbs turned to wings and claws, skin to feathers, mouths to beaks. They had all become birds. Grandpa John had changed into some sort of bird of prey, while Mrs Pal had turned into a crane. And at the head of the table screamed a brilliant blue-and-green peacock, its tail flaring.

The only consolation for Spencer was that he, Max and Stan were unchanged. But so was Beatrice.

'Can you understand what they're saying, Stan?' asked Max over the cacophony of birds' whistles and cries.

'I don't speak bird!' Stan sounded a trifle offended at the suggestion, although right at that moment Chit and Chat swooped from the chandelier to settle upon his antlers.

Spotting Beatrice peering out from behind her hands, Spencer shouted fiercely, 'Turn them back!'

'I don't know how!' Beatrice said, tears in her eyes. 'I didn't even know my dad *had* such a thing. It must only work on adults.'

'You'd better spill everything you do know, right now.'

Beatrice hunched over miserably on the floor, looking very small. 'You're going to hate me. But I promise I didn't know all this would happen.'

She crawled to Max, then gingerly reached into his massive thatch of hair and pulled out a tiny bone, a bit like a knobbly door handle, less than a centimetre long.

'How did you know that was in there?' Max said, looking at the bone suspiciously.

'I hid it in there.'

'Why?'

'So I could eavesdrop on you guys. It's like a spy microphone but, you know, magic.'

Outraged, Max sprang away from Beatrice and vigorously ran his hands through his hair to flush out any other hidden contraptions. Two jelly magicians fell out, left over from their game in Beatrice's blanket fort kitchen.

'I knew it,' Stan snorted, stamping a hoof. 'Didn't I tell you she was fishier than salted cod? Get to the door, Spencer and Maxwell, I shall protect your flank as we retreat!'

'No, don't go!' cried Beatrice. 'I heard what your

grandfather said about Albert Nobody, and what he did to your family. I swear I knew nothing about him being so . . . hostile. At first, I thought all he wanted was to help me in the tournament. But I guess he was using me. Everything snowballed because my grandfather is going to try to get the Loom.'

Hugging her knees, Beatrice told them what she knew. Decades ago, her grandfather had learnt that he was suffering from a very serious illness, one that his doctors had thought could not be cured. Determined to somehow survive, Nobody had used magic to sever his spirit and mind from his body. He was still alive now in this bizarre way, but without a form to call his own.

Over the years, Nobody came to believe it had been a grave mistake to give up his body like that, sick though it was. His spirit and mind couldn't hold together for ever without a form in which to reside. Since being freed from his chandelier prison, the *trujuklinkot* at Hoarder Hill, he had tried enduring without form, but freedom had turned out to be a curse. If he didn't bind in something or someone, he would be nothing but a senseless fragment, haunting without purpose.

But taking over other bodies didn't feel right. It was like wearing ill-fitting clothes, even though they started to resemble Nobody's old appearance. Worst of all was the frightened or angry – sometimes both frightened *and* angry – spirit of the person to whom the body really belonged, suppressed in a dark place inside but always fighting to get Nobody out.

So Albert Nobody wanted to undo his unbearable decision by changing his past. Verdandi's Loom, weaver of time, was his plan to do that.

'He got me to send a note on Mr Rabble's letter-head,' Beatrice went on wretchedly, 'telling your grandad and Mrs Pal that Rabble had information about your grandad's mirror map. And once he knew you were here, he told me to help you find out what you could about the map. Rabble wasn't the one who told the Sleight about the map. It was me.'

'No wonder you were so nosy about Hedy and the map tattoos,' said Spencer. 'You were trying to get information out of me and Max.'

'No! It wasn't just that. I *like* spending time with you guys.' She rubbed her eyes with a fist. 'I heard what your grandad said about changing people's fates. I'm afraid of what will happen if my grandfather uses the

Loom. What if it means *I* change, or am never even born?'

'If you don't want to find out,' said Stan, 'you need to help us stop him. How is he going to try to get the Loom?'

'The Sleight asked Rabble to make Bess a slipway to the next location on the map,' said Beatrice. 'When Bess went to Pick Pocket Parlour, I had one of the Theries slip the pocket watch into Bess's pack. My grandfather is hiding in the pocket watch.'

'I thought the Theries *picked* pockets, not put things *into* pockets,' scoffed Max.

Beatrice shrugged. 'They'll do either. If you pay them.'

'So,' said Spencer, 'now Bess is trying to intercept my sister and your grandfather is hiding out on Bess.' He covered his head with his hands to think. He wished that Hedy was here to tell him what to do, but when he checked the telejotter there was still no new message from her. Spencer hastily wrote: *Hedy, Grandpa John and Mrs Pal have been turned into birds. And Nobody is trying to get the Loom. He's hiding on Bess. Be careful!*

He glared at Beatrice. 'How can we undo this bird

spell? Don't forget your own dad is stuck like that unless we figure it out.'

'I told you, I don't know how!' She paused. 'But maybe Mr Rabble does.'

Rabble blinked at Stan, not quite believing what he was seeing.

'Are you a chimera?' he asked the stag. 'I've never heard of a deer–parrot hybrid before. Hasn't got the same *dynamism* as a gryphon or a manticore. What do they call you?'

'We are not a chimera, sir,' Stan said very stiffly. '*I* am a stag that happens to be accompanied by birds.'

They had done their best to sneak into Pick Pocket Parlour without drawing attention, but eyes had followed them all the way to Rabble's booth. In painstaking detail they explained everything to the old magician – Nobody intent on the Loom, Hedy and the others on their quest in the Slip, the grown-ups all turning into birds – but it was proving difficult to keep his thoughts on track.

'Can you help us, Mr Rabble?' Spencer asked, trying to get the muddled man back to business.

'Eh?'

'Can you help turn my grandad and Mrs Pal back to humans? And stop Nobody?'

Rabble frowned. 'One cannot be everywhere at once. We shall have to divide and conquer.'

'We?' Spencer's heart began to pitter-patter.

'You've pinpointed the two things that need to be done. You're of no use for one of them, but you're the very best placed for the other. You need to stop Albert. And I will attend to the *avian* situation.' He flapped his hands a little, as though it were a game.

'*We* need to stop Albert Nobody?' Spencer repeated.

'Now's not the time to shirk, lad. You seem to know more about him than anyone else.' Rabble settled his gaze on Beatrice. 'And you're his granddaughter? I'm rather hurt you never told me so. Well, my dear, *you* are especially powerful in the matter of pinning down your grandfather's spirit. You must summon him with these words: *By blood and bone, I call you out. By blood and bone, I call you in. By blood and bone, I call you down.* And you must mean it – you must have every ounce of your being behind the intent of those words.'

'Can I summon him from here?' Beatrice asked apprehensively.

'Not possible. You'll need to get within eyesight and earshot of him.'

Spencer sighed hopelessly. 'How do we do that? We'll never catch up to Hedy and Jelly, even if we could find where they went into the Slip.'

'You won't catch up to them if you follow in their footsteps. You'll need a shortcut.' Rabble smiled widely. 'I may be ancient and forced into retirement but, as the Sleight knows, I'm still the best Slip engineer here at the Fantastikhana. Just ask Bess.'

## CHAPTER 22

## A CAVE OF MELODY

Without opening her eyes, Hedy knew that she was lying on hard rock, she was sodden, and she was cold.

Nearby, Jelly and Cyrus were stirring, and Doug was already sitting up. With a start, Hedy remembered the last moments before everything went dark – the dizzying whirlpool, the Kelpie King, the bubble, and—! She relaxed her clenched fingers. The ring of quartz was there in her palm. And on the back of her hand, the silvery symbol had changed to ≈.

Her backpack was still on. She carefully packed the

round stone away and then inspected everything inside. Verdandi's frame was still safe and sound in her sweater but, to her amazement, it had doubled in size. The telejotter was waterlogged, its pages stuck together and unusable.

They were in a cave somewhere. The entire place, including the rocks on which they had awoken, seemed to be made of columns of hexagonal stone. Not too far away, she could see the cave entrance opening out to the sea and sky, so they weren't underground any more.

Below their ledge was a channel that allowed the swell of the sea to wash in and out. The waves echoed off the ceiling and walls with the whooshing of the wind, rebounding and layering to create a sound that was almost choir-like. She closed her eyes and fixed her mind on the pull of the map.

'The map tattoos want us to go that way,' Hedy said, pointing to the horizon beyond the cave entrance.

Cyrus lifted a finger to his lips, then indicated the channel below. Jelly's clog canoe drifted back and forth in the water, although the paddles were gone. Not far away lay Bess, face down on the rocks, a hand gripping his pack. His chest was rising and falling; he was alive.

One of his legs was still partly sheathed with stalactite from the Kelpie King's cave, like a cast of stone.

'That'll slow him down, when he comes around,' said Cyrus.

They crept as quietly as they could to the canoe, and hopped in, the wind gusting around them, making the cave sing and their teeth chatter with cold.

But when Hedy put her hand on the rim of the canoe, nothing happened. The map tattoos definitely wanted her to travel out through the cave entrance and out to sea, but there was no pull as there had been in the slipstream. 'We'll have to paddle,' she told the others.

'Not the way,' said a weak voice. It was Bess, who had awoken and was pushing himself up with a hand.

'What do you mean it's not the way?' Hedy asked. 'I can feel it.'

'Trust me, you'll be paddling for ever. Lucky if you don't get blown off course and drown.'

'We'd sooner trust a viper than you,' Doug growled.

Bess wheezed, amused. 'Zero to no vipers here in the Cave of Melody, so I'm all you've got. If you help me break this stalactite from my leg, I'll tell you how we're going to raise the slipway.'

Jelly shot the treasure hunter her most withering mean-girl look. 'We're not stupid. You're here to make sure we don't get the Loom. Tell us how, and *then* we might help you with your leg.'

'No deal,' said Bess flatly.

But something struck Hedy about how he'd described where they were. *Cave of Melody*. It set off an itch in her brain, as though the answer was something she already knew, if only she could remember. As the wind eddied around the cave, creating that choir-like sound, Hedy recalled the song that the storm kelpies had been singing before the whirlpool had sucked them down:

*Sing yellow, sing blue, sing red, sing green,*
*That's how the slipway shall be seen!*
*Jump yellow, jump blue, jump green, jump red,*
*Run where the giants feared to tread!*

'That's how the slipway shall be seen,' Hedy whispered to herself. She lifted up her face and softly tried out the first lines of the storm kelpies' song.

The wind whipped the words from her lips and swirled them around the cave, echoing over and over tantalizingly before dying out. *Again, louder*, Hedy told herself. With a deep breath, she sang it again.

The wind seemed to sigh in pleasure and bore the song to every nook and cranny of the cave. As the echoes whirled and layered into a choir of Hedys, colours began to glow just beneath the channel water. They were the tops of hexagonal columns that were too short to break the surface: a yellow, a blue, a green and a red.

Elated, Hedy scrambled out of the canoe, followed by the others. 'Don't need a Bess when you've got a Hedy,' Doug gloated.

'What now?' Jelly asked, scanning the colours under the water.

Cyrus murmured the words of the song. '*Jump yellow, jump blue, jump green, jump red.*' Then he launched himself on to the yellow glow with a splash. 'Blue,' he called next, making the leap to the blue.

'Green's pretty far,' said Hedy, pointing to the further colour about two metres away from him.

But for Cyrus, with his half-fae abilities, the distance was easy. He bounced to the green glow, and then the red.

*Crack. Boom.*

The cave shook. From beneath the sea surface emerged a mighty bridge of those same hexagonal columns, leading from the mouth of the cave out to sea. The map tattoos in Hedy danced in her skin, tugging her towards it. This was their path.

'Hedy! Cyrus!' called Bess as they began to pick their way to the mouth of the cave.

Cyrus stopped. He thought for a moment, and then began to backtrack.

'What are you doing?' asked Hedy.

'Making sure we get a good head start. Here, give me the troll's whisker. Don't worry, I'm only going to tie him up, not going to put his head under water or anything.'

Hedy felt a surprising pang of regret as she handed the whisker to him. Even though the very notion of it was still a bit repulsive, it was unique, and it was hers.

As Cyrus drew closer to Bess, the treasure hunter tried to drag himself away and cover his ears. But it was no good. Cyrus crooned a sleepy melody that itself echoed gently through the cave, until Bess drooped and fell still.

The bridge of basalt columns – which they quickly nicknamed Hexagon Bridge – rose about three metres above the water, and was nearly as wide as a football field. Great swells crashed against the columns, misting them with sea spray. It was unnerving to be walking out here, over the middle of the sea.

Everyone but Doug felt the cold on the bridge with nothing to cut the wind. Hedy walked alongside the bear as closely as she could, her arms wrapped around her, and her head down against the stiff breeze. Seabirds wheeled overhead, and behind her was the regular *klok klok* of Jelly's clogs; Cyrus had shrunk their 'canoe' back down to its original state before they'd set out.

Slip magic must have been at work on the Hexagon Bridge, just as it had been in the tunnels on land, but out here it was easier to spot. To the east were hazy dark patches on the horizon – land, maybe Scotland – and every now and then the patches would unexpectedly change position, as though miles had been covered in just a few steps.

'Squirrel nuts, what is that?' Doug exclaimed as something huge and grey breached the surface of the water and let out a great wheeze.

'That was a whale,' Hedy replied, awed. They all paused, humbly watching the massive creature and hoping that it wouldn't develop a destructive curiosity about the bridge that had suddenly appeared in its territory.

'A *whale*? It's enormous.'

'Could your Snowy Paw of Doom take it on, Doug?' teased Jelly.

Doug blanched. 'I've never seen a creature so big.'

'I think there are bigger whales than that, too,' Hedy said.

'In that case, I'll stick to land creatures.'

Despite the cold, Hedy was wonderstruck by the majesty of the moment – the horizon, the whale, the massive bridge stretching so far ahead. Who else had been here to take in the world like this? She looked back the way they had come, to see how small the cave now looked. What she saw made her gulp: in the distance, a small black figure.

Bess must have come round and freed himself, and now he was on their trail.

## CHAPTER 23

## THE PACT

They ran. It was slippery on the Hexagon Bridge, and after a few minutes Jelly had to take off her clogs and run as best she could in her thick socks. Only Cyrus, longing to use his bounce, could keep up the pace. He was visibly frustrated when they had to slow down because Doug ran out of puff ('Bears aren't made for long-distance chases,' he gasped), Hedy got a stitch in her side, or Jelly's feet were sore. As soon as they got their breath, Cyrus urged them all into a jog again. But the basalt columns ran straight ahead for ages, offering nowhere to hide, and Bess drew nearer and nearer, as relentless as a machine.

'We're never going to outrun him,' Hedy panted eventually. Bess was only a few hundred metres behind them now.

'Then we'll have to stop him,' said Cyrus.

'What do you mean?'

Cyrus halted. 'We have to face him head on.'

Within minutes, Bess was just a few metres away. He was breathing deeply, but otherwise appeared like he could have chased them down all day. All remnants of the stalactite were gone, and the troll's whisker was coiled at his hip.

Without warning, Cyrus launched himself at Bess, a full-pelt run that knocked the hawk-nosed man over. Grunting, they grappled and scrapped, then fell and rolled over and over towards the side of the bridge. Finally, Bess, heavier and obviously skilled at fighting, overpowered Cyrus and pinned him down, holding the teenager's hands behind his back.

'Are you done, Cy?' Bess asked. He seemed to have stuffed precautionary tissue in his ears, because he was nearly shouting.

Cyrus, who now sported a small gash on his chin, glared daggers at the treasure hunter.

'Don't be like that,' said Bess condescendingly. 'I'm just trying to deter you from acts of ignorance and stupidity.'

'Let him go,' shouted Hedy.

'Not until you promise not to be ignorant or stupid.'

'We're neither!'

'You sure about that?'

'What do you mean?'

'Cyrus means to use the Loom, doesn't he?' When no one denied it, Bess knew he had hit home. 'The Sleight aren't as dim-witted as you think, Cyrus. You want to use it to get to the Aos Sí lands, don't you?'

'So?' Cyrus twisted in Bess's grip, trying to get his arm free.

'If you use it, it could mean the destruction of the Fantastikhana.'

At that, the fight leaked out of Cyrus. Bess released his arm and backed away, pulling the tissue from his ears.

'Why would it destroy the Fantastikhana?' growled Doug.

Bess poked about in his pack and withdrew a few pieces of cloth patterned with matchsticks. He held them out to the little group. 'These are wintertide ties.

Hang them around your necks to warm up and dry off a bit.'

'We're not cold,' Hedy lied.

'Just put them on,' said Bess wearily. 'I don't want you falling over from exposure while I explain everything. It's not a trap – look.' And he pulled a scrap of the same cloth from inside his own shirt.

They put them on – Hedy tied one around Doug's thick neck – and welcome heat immediately radiated from where the cloth lay against them. Standing in a huddle in the middle of the sea, they listened to the treasure hunter.

'Generations ago,' said Bess, 'a pact was made between magicians and non-magicians.'

'You mean bogs like us?' said Jelly.

Bess's mouth twitched. 'Yes, bogs like you. And me. Magicians back then were powerful, you see. But people without magical talent, who had no access to magical objects, became jealous and afraid. Jealous of the power, afraid of what they didn't know, afraid of what magicians might be able to do.'

Hedy leant in closer. Despite her misgivings about Bess, she knew he was unveiling something gravely important. 'What sort of things?'

'The Slip, for instance,' said Bess. 'They were afraid that magicians would find a way to heaven or paradise or something of that nature. If a way to such a place had been found, it might have undermined thousands of years of teaching by certain *institutions*. That's why travel through all but a very small part of the Slip is now forbidden. We bogs were so afraid we'd lose our own power that we tried to wipe out magic.'

Although Bess had said 'we', Hedy had a hard time thinking of him as anything like the fearful, jealous non-magicians he was describing.

'Many great creations were destroyed,' Bess continued, 'and others were hidden to protect them, like this gloriously troublesome Loom. Before magicians were extinguished, they came to an agreement with the other side: the Pact. They agreed to conceal themselves instead of being eradicated. Magic could endure, as long as it was hidden, as long as it did not openly flourish. Real magic can be performed as long as it is believed to be only an illusion. *But*, if the Pact is ever broken, then the other side will try to stamp out the Fantastikhana. They'll collapse the cavern, the libraries, the active slipways. Because the Fantastikhana isn't just a children's competition. It's a chance for the magician community to get together and exchange knowledge, to experiment, to celebrate the youngsters of the future. In other words: to flourish. The other side would love a chance to outlaw it.'

Hedy shivered and leant into Doug's side.

'The other side have just enough monitoring in place to make life difficult. Use of something as powerful as the Loom could be detected, and they may accuse magicians of breaking the Pact.'

'What's wrong with the blinking Sleight?' growled Doug. 'If they'd just explain this to everyone, we might not be freezing our ears off in the middle of the sea out here.'

Bess turned to the bear gravely. 'Not all magicians have good intentions. Not all magicians care about the community. There are those who work solely for their own glory and wouldn't give two figs if everyone else was stamped out.' He took a deep breath. 'I'm not on this assignment for fortune or glory. I'm here to make sure you spirited young dunderheads don't use the Loom.'

Steam rose from their damp clothes and fur as they considered what Bess had just told them. Hedy felt like the two pieces of Verdandi's Loom in her backpack were ticking time bombs waiting to be detonated. She looked sidelong at Cyrus and said softly, 'We can't use the Loom if it will destroy the Fantastikhana.'

Cyrus's eyes were on the horizon, and his mouth was a hard line, trying not to crumple. 'If you're saying not to use the Loom, you're saying I can't go back to my people. I dwindle into a nobody without magic, so that everyone else can practise their pathetic version in secret, like always.'

Bess said, 'You're not without people here, Cyrus. And you wouldn't be without magic either.'

'The Sleight aren't *family*, Bess. They're a child-rearing board. And the magic they want me to learn? Imagine having your wings clipped and being told, *Don't worry, just try jumping really high*. It's nothing like the same. Oh, but you probably can't even imagine that. You're just a giftless bog tracker.'

Cyrus stalked away to the edge of the bridge. When Jelly took a step after him, Bess murmured, 'Give the boy a moment.' Jelly crossed her arms with a mulish expression on her face, but stayed where she was.

'That's mine,' Hedy muttered, pointing to the troll whisker at Bess's hip.

'Well, you lot basically gave it to me,' said Bess,

resting a hand on top of the coiled whisker like it was a holster. He laughed at Hedy's black scowl. 'One thing you'll have to learn about a troll's whisker is that it won't commit to cruel acts. Knots in it won't hold a captive for long. You'll need ordinary rope for that.'

'I'll remember that,' said Hedy stiffly.

Not bothering to hide his mocking smile, Bess bowed his head. 'Thank you for saving me from the Kelpie King's cave. If you hadn't freed me, that would have been the end of my tale.'

He untied the whisker from his hip and held it out to Hedy. As she crammed it into her backpack, she half-wished she had a belt like Bess so she could wear it as he had done. After seeing him handle it, the whisker didn't seem as gross as it had before.

'How can you be so calm?' she asked. 'When you were going to be encased in rock for the rest of your life?'

'I don't think the rest of my life was going to be much longer,' he said. He pulled a compass from his pocket, checked the position of the sun, then nodded in Cyrus's direction. 'Speaking of much longer, how long do you think he's going to brood? We should get going.'

Thawed out by the wintertide ties, they continued their march along the Hexagon Bridge. Cyrus was so morose and withdrawn that even Jelly decided to give him some time alone.

Despite her earlier misgivings, Hedy found herself very curious about the treasure hunter pacing alongside them. 'What's your real name?' she asked.

'I only answer to Bess these days,' he said. 'Treasure hunters see it as an honour to have the title, you know. It's for Bess Houdini, the wife of Harry Houdini.' He half-turned to check on Cyrus trudging behind them. 'You know what infuriates me about Lord Misery Guts back there? He knows so much that he's well ahead of many older magicians still kicking around. Candice and Flora have been teaching him almost from the moment they saw his prophecy. But he's too busy moaning about his clipped wings to put in some hard yards. So what if your gift isn't what it used to be? *I* don't have any gifts at all, and I'm still having fun.'

'How did you become a treasure hunter?'

'By being a little punk with a chip on his shoulder. I loved magic stuff, but wasn't any good at manipulating it. Not like, say, your grandfather. So I felt like I had to prove myself. But I do like using ready-made tools that makers produce. And I'm good at finding the old lost things.'

It was the first time Hedy had seen Bess look actually happy, rather than mocking.

'OK, I have a *zillion* questions,' said Jelly. 'What's the most exciting place you've gone hunting for treasure? And what's the most exciting thing you've found? And what do you do with them?'

'How about the creatures you've come across,' Doug added. 'Any other talking bears on your travels?'

As they peppered Bess with questions, Hedy paused and turned to make sure Cyrus was OK. He had stopped in his tracks, and was holding a knuckle to the cut on his chin.

'Cyrus?' Hedy called out, troubled.

A streak of blue light flickered over him, and a cold tremor of dread ran down Hedy's spine. The colour was all too familiar. It was the same shade of blue that had signalled Albert Nobody at Hoarder Hill. *No*, she thought, *it can't be, how can it be, please don't let it be.* Because when her Uncle Peter had been wounded by exploding glass, when the magpie Therie had suffered a cut to its wing, Nobody had been able to take them over. *Please don't let it be.*

Cyrus opened his mouth and began to sing that crooning lullaby that he'd used to knock out Bess back at the Cave of Melody. His voice was lifted by the wind, and washed over all their ears, bringing with it a deep, sinking sleep.

## CHAPTER 24

## SHORTCUT

'Who's going first?' Rabble wheezed, standing back from the dusty Slip entrance that he had just opened up.

A short while before, Spencer, Max, Beatrice and Stan had followed him into the cellar of Pick Pocket Parlour. He seemed to have some arrangement with the manager, who had waved them through a scarred door without argument. At Rabble's direction, the children had shifted a few empty barrels to clear space in front of a wall.

Rabble had then taken a tiny sledgehammer – only

as long as a finger – and tapped it lightly on the masonry. The mortar had crumbled and the stone blocks had fallen away, revealing a dark passageway. 'Shouldn't have bothered bricking it up after Bess,' he now murmured.

'Where does it go?' Spencer asked, shrinking back.

'It's your shortcut to catch up with your sisters.' Rabble hastily began to write on a scrap of paper from his pocket. 'I'm going to give you some directions, and you'd better follow them carefully, otherwise who knows where you might end up. The first portion of this slipway is well established – hardly ever used now, of course, but stable. I'll be nudging open a new slip-way for you, from Belfast. I'm guessing you could make it in an hour or so.' He thrust the scrap of paper to Spencer, who took it with shaking fingers.

'We can't see in the tunnel,' said Spencer. Why did his voice sound so squeaky?

Max suddenly yanked Spencer's sleeve in excitement. 'Don't you remember what Ewan showed us Chit and Chat could do? Chit and Chat, light up, please!'

Cool yellow light swept over the tunnel as the cockatoos lifted their wings and lit up their crests. They all blinked at the sudden illumination.

Spencer checked the telejotter again, but there was still no word from Hedy. They couldn't waste any more time. 'Thank you, Mr Rabble.'

The old man nodded. 'Hurry on, now. I'll get that slipway ready for you.'

Spencer hoped Rabble was clear-headed enough to do it correctly. He hoped the directions Rabble had given them were good enough. He hoped Hedy and Jelly and Doug were all right, and he'd be able to find them, and that Hedy could tell him what to do. Clinging to these hopes like a life raft, he led the others into the Slip tunnel.

They edged along the slipway slowly at first, and then more confidently, easily avoiding the occasional wayward tree roots that poked down.

'I always thought that pocket watch was my lucky charm,' Beatrice said softly. 'Everything started going well for me when it turned up. I was so sure I could finish the Fantastikhana at least in third place! I won't be winning anything now, and I won't be getting a mentor and I'll be stuck with fuddled old Rabble – if he'll even take me back, that is. *And* if the Sleight don't ban me or put me in a dungeon somewhere.'

'They won't put you in a dungeon if we stop Nobody,' Spencer told her.

That familiar obstinate look came over Beatrice. 'We're making a mistake, you know. I'm a loser without that pocket watch. What if I can't stop my grandfather?'

Spencer wondered if he should tell her that of course she could do it, that he believed in her. He supposed that was the motivation she needed. But in fact, he had no idea if Albert Nobody being in the pocket watch had made a difference to her ability and her tournament placings. And he didn't honestly know if he trusted her either. But now was not the time to be hopeless, or helpless, so he said the only sincere thing that he could think of. 'We have to at least try.'

Hanging her head, Beatrice said, 'You know, I found out that my dad tried to steal from Mrs Pal. He tried to break into Mrs Pal's shop to steal the map tattoos. But now I think it wasn't really him. I think my grandfather took over him and made him do it.'

Spencer stumbled at her words. That made sense of why Ned had always acted so strangely around Mrs

Pal. 'She said the intruder had fallen off her roof. Is that how your dad broke his arm?'

She nodded. 'What if my grandfather does the same to me, Spence? What if I'm the wrong person to stop him?'

Spencer looked her in the eye and said again, 'We have to at least try.'

'Stars and moon, I believe I came down this very passageway the last time I was at the Fantastikhana,' said Stan as they reached a junction branching in four directions.

One tunnel was marked Belfast, one was labelled Newfoundland and Labrador ('A land of dogs?' Max asked, but Beatrice said, 'No, just Canada.'), and the other said it was bound for Tangier via Lisbon. The fourth tunnel, a new-looking one to the right of the Belfast tunnel, had no name at all. That must be the new slipway Mr Rabble had made for them.

'Look,' Stan cried. He trotted forwards to study the Belfast insignia, a painting of a wolf and a seahorse. 'Yes, I remember accidentally marking this wolf here with my antler – see that scrape?' The deer looked longingly down the tunnel that ultimately led to

Tangier. 'A prior master brought me from that direction, so I suppose my old forest is somewhere that way. My old home, back when I still looked like this.'

Spencer could feel Stan's urge to head that way. But the stag shook it off and backed away from the Tangier tunnel. 'My home is with your grandfather and Rose now, isn't it? I'm not like what I was back then.' He turned around to face the nameless tunnel. 'Find the wolf and seahorse and turn right. That's the way Rabble said to go, isn't it?'

The new slipway was more roughly cut than the passageway they had walked along so far, its walls more jagged, its ceiling uneven in height. But it only took about ten minutes before it began sloping upwards. A trace of the sea blew along the slipway. And then came the far-off sound of waves, and around a bend the blush of daylight. The exit was close.

'Come on!' cried Spencer, picking up the pace.

Perfect blue skies met them as they emerged from the slipway on to a rocky coastline. Tens of thousands of hexagonal stone columns and their worn-down remnants stretched along the water's edge. Behind them rose steep grassy cliffs, and the scene was empty of people. There was no sign of the girls, Doug or Cyrus.

'Hedy?' Spencer called, scanning up and down the shore.

'I'd bet an antler that they're somewhere out there,' said Stan. The stag nodded in the direction of a vast pier that ran like an endless road out to sea, also made of hexagonal stone columns. 'I think that's the Causeway. And I think we've beaten them here.'

'What do we do? Go out there to find them?'

Stan looked nervous but said, 'I'll never hear the end of it from that braggart bear if I don't go and see what it's like. Very well, then. Let's go and find them.'

They began to cautiously make their way towards the start of the Causeway. Close to the water's edge, they passed one massive column atop of which was a rusty, curling funnel. Its trumpet end was as tall as Spencer and pointed out to sea. Max, as excited as a dog off its leash, darted up the pillars that led to the horn.

'There are some words up here,' he called.

'What do they say?' Spencer asked.

'*This mighty cla*—. . . Oh, I don't know what that word is.' He shrugged, and before anyone could stop him, he put his lips to the mouthpiece of the instrument, puffed out his cheeks and blew into it.

A deep, resounding tone rang out from the horn, far more powerful than Spencer would have guessed from the instrument's derelict appearance. He raced up the pillar steps, yelling at Max to stop.

'Why? Now Jelly and Hedy will know we're here.'

'We don't want *other* people to know we're here, though. And how would they know it's us, anyway?'

At the base of the instrument were the words that Max had been too lazy to read, carved into the stone.

*This mighty clarion shall appear,*
*When Verdandi's frame and stone are near.*
*Sound it if you seek the thread*
*Of fate. Then run the race as read.*

A chill ran over Spencer as he took in the words. He felt sure that Max had triggered something that he shouldn't have, something that Spencer had no idea how to handle. 'Come on, and don't touch, or blow, or break *anything.*'

As they stole along the shore towards the Causeway, a swathe of fog began to form on the horizon. 'I don't like the look of that,' muttered Stan. 'Where did it come from? And why is it growing so fast?'

He was right. The fog was swelling with unnatural speed, outwards and upwards.

They rounded the headland into a bay, where the cliffs curved in a steep half-bowl. The Causeway started here, slicing the bay in half as it jutted out to sea. There was no sign of the girls, Doug or Cyrus here either.

'I'm not walking out there,' Beatrice said, her eyes fixed on the sky.

The fog was no longer a fog. It was an ominous tower of cloud blotting out the sun. Spencer had learnt about clouds at school, and his favourite type by far had been *cumulonimbus* because they were known as thunderheads. This looming cloud was most definitely a thunderhead: spectacular, dense, and with a flat anvil shape at the top. The anvil was pointed straight at them, which, Spencer anxiously remembered, meant a storm was coming their way.

'OK. Maybe . . .' Spencer faltered and looked around the empty bay. 'Maybe we should shelter here until the storm passes.'

As they began to retreat from the water, lightning flashed around the thunderhead cloud, and from over the clifftop came a sound of pounding.

## CHAPTER 25

## FROM INSIDE THE THUNDERHEAD

The children and Stan ran for a huge boulder at the headland, feeling the ground beneath them shake. And then, over the top of the cliff leapt giants. Around thirty of them – male and female – some lanky, some podgy, most of them as tall as a four-storey building. There were even a couple of giant children.

The crowd settled themselves into the grassy half-bowl cliff that formed a natural amphitheatre, with the air of spectators getting ready for a big game. A girl giant (if Spencer had to guess, he would have said she was around eight) asked, 'What's that pathway out to sea, Mama?'

'That's the bridge all the way from Fingal's Cave,' said her mother. 'Must be a mighty magician. No one's raised that before.'

'Where is she, then?' said the girl giant. 'I want to see the mighty magician. Oh, look!'

The girl giant had left her spot on the cliff face to find the magician that they were all expecting, and unfortunately had spotted three children, two cocka-toos and a stag peering fearfully from behind a massive rock. 'I found her!'

The giants jumped to their feet, and pushed and shoved each other to get a look at them. Spencer had never felt so miniscule in his whole life.

'What's that one?' asked a giant, pointing a massive finger at Max. 'The one with the fuzzy head and face. A bigfoot?'

'What's a bigfoot?' said the girl.

'A creature in the Americas. Hairy blighters. I guess his foot don't look big enough to be a bigfoot.'

'I'm going to speak giant to them,' Max said under his breath.

'What?' Spencer said.

Max puffed out his chest and shouted, 'Fee, fie, fo, fum! I smell the blood of an Englishman!'

Spencer groaned. The last thing they should be doing was putting blood on these giants' minds. But the massive faces simply looked at him, blank and uncomprehending.

'What's he on about?' said the one who thought Max was a bigfoot.

'No blinkin' idea,' muttered another.

'Their deer looks mighty delicious,' said the very biggest giant, smacking his lips. 'Juicy and fat.'

'Fat?' Stan bristled. 'I'm a stag in his prime! Strong and seasoned. Magnificent muscles.'

'Shush, Stan,' Spencer hissed, 'you'll make them want to eat you even more.'

'You don't look old enough to be a full magician,' the girl giant said to Beatrice.

Beatrice shook her head and mumbled, 'I'm not a full magician.'

'So, you won't be racing?' the girl pouted. And then her eyes fell on Spencer's red hair. 'Oh, it's a lucky ginger, Mama! Maybe he's the one who's racing!'

The thunderhead cloud had twisted closer to the shoreline, covering the Causeway. With a deafening crack, a fissure appeared at its base. Footsteps boomed inside, and all the giants scrambled back to their spots in their amphitheatre as though the show was starting.

'Who sounded the foghorn?' roared a voice from inside the thunderhead.

Out of the fissure emerged a bearded man about three or four metres tall – nowhere near as huge as the creatures sitting in the cliff face. He bulged with muscles, however, as though he had been squished into a too-small casing. The watching giants whooped at his arrival like he was a champion fighter, cheering, 'Gint! Gint! Gint!'

The half-giant, who wore only one shoe, lapped it up, even egged them on. 'Who sounded the foghorn?' he bellowed again.

'One of *them* did,' shouted a giant, waving a hand at Spencer and the others cowering on the headland. 'I'll wager a cow that it was the ginger one.'

The half-giant peered at them. 'That's nearly a whole sleight of magicians there,' he said. 'Which one of you is the challenger? Or are all of you having a go?'

The children and Stan were too dumbfounded to say a word. Chit, however, screeched, 'Challenger?'

'Have a go!' squawked Chat.

'Come on, one or all of you?' the half-giant said. 'I can't be waiting all day.'

'I will!'

All heads – human, animal and giant – swivelled to the end of the Causeway, as a figure fought its way through the swirling cloud. 'I will challenge you!'

It was Cyrus.

Spencer felt a rush of relief. If Cyrus was there, that meant Hedy was nearby. 'Cyrus!' he called out, waving.

Cyrus hesitated a moment, squinted, then waved back.

'Very well. Gront? What are you doing, sitting up there on your colossal backside? We need you to read out the rules of the race!'

The very biggest giant, who looked none too intelligent, heaved to his feet and began to clamber down. 'All right, Gint, I'm on my way.'

'Hurry up, brother,' scolded Gint. 'Where's the scroll with the rules?'

Gront pulled from his pocket a very official-looking scroll, about the size of a large bin. 'Gint, did you see that delicious-looking deer over there?' he whispered at a volume only slightly lower than that of a loudspeaker. 'Can I have him if you win the race?'

'I don't know if that's in the rules,' said Gint.

Gront whipped a pencil almost a metre long from another pocket. 'What if I write it into the rules?' He started scribbling at once, ignoring Stan's outraged protests.

'Got a problem with that, young magician?' Gint asked.

'He can put it in,' called Cyrus. 'Because you're not going to win the race. What are the rules, anyway? You haven't told me yet.'

Gront cleared his throat and held the scroll before him. 'Here be the official rules for the race for Verdandi's thread. You beat Gint, you win. Whizzballs are allowed. And . . . if Gint wins, his brother Gront gets to keep the stag.' He rolled the scroll back up.

'That's it?' Cyrus frowned.

Gront nodded. 'That's it.'

'What are whizzballs?' Spencer asked. He looked around keenly for a sign of Hedy, but decided against asking Cyrus. Perhaps Hedy was hiding for a reason.

'They just make the race a bit more exciting, that's all,' said Gront evasively. 'Now, Gint, why are you wearing only one shoe? Ma's going to rip your ear off if you've lost it.'

'I haven't lost it, you numbskull, and don't you go telling Ma that I have. It's right there, hiding in front of the ginger-haired magician and the hairy gnome and your delicious deer snack.'

Gint pointed at the rock behind which they stood, and they all backed away. From a distance, Spencer realized that their rock was the shape of a large boot – a boot as tall as a grown-up, and as long and wide as a bed.

'You can't run in that!' Max scoffed. 'It reaches your belly!'

'Does it, now, furry goblin?' smiled Gint. He stomped towards them, and then stuck his thumb in his mouth. Huffing and puffing, Gint the half-giant began to blow himself up. With each breath, he sprouted upwards, outwards, skywards, until he was even taller than Gront.

The children and Stan scampered away from the rock boot. Now that Gint was so massive, it looked a good fit for his grubby foot. Laces appeared in the rock, and he picked it up to slide it on as easily as a leather shoe.

They dashed to the Causeway to join Cyrus. 'Where are Hedy and Jelly and Doug?' Spencer whispered urgently.

Cyrus scanned the Causeway, although the thunder-head cloud still cut much of it from view. 'They couldn't keep up with me. I ran ahead.'

'Are they OK?'

Cyrus nodded. He looked at their motley little group for a long moment. 'How did you get here?'

'Mr Rabble helped us. Did Bess find you?'

But there was no more time to talk. Gint stomped to the water's edge, stretching to show off his muscles. 'It's time to race, challenger,' he said to Cyrus with a crafty grin.

## CHAPTER 26

## THE GIANT'S CAUSEWAY

Hedy was the first to awaken, roused by the urgent drag of the map tattoos. She flinched when thunder clapped overhead; she'd never been that close to it before. It seemed to stir the columns of the bridge.

She struggled up, heavy-eyed and heavy-limbed, trying to make sense of what was happening. The pillars around them were sinking into the sea. Behind them, towards the Cave of Melody, the bridge was disappearing, and there was no more bridge in front of them either. She, Jelly, Doug and Bess were lying on a small island of stone pillars in the middle of the sea. Cyrus was gone.

Far ahead there seemed to be a different bridge running through the sea. Either her eyes were tricking her, or it was rising and falling. That was where the map wanted her to go.

When she saw her backpack was unbuckled, Hedy knew what would be missing, but with a leaden stomach she checked anyway. Then she shook the others awake.

'Cyrus took the Loom pieces,' she said. 'He sang us to sleep so he could steal them.'

'Why would he do that?' Jelly moaned, massaging her head.

'I think somehow Albert Nobody has taken over him.' It seemed so improbable when Hedy said it aloud. And yet, Cyrus had that cut on his chin, and she was sure she had spotted that tell-tale blue light.

'Albert Nobody?' said Bess thickly. 'The dead magician who could take off his head?'

'He's not dead enough, I'll tell you that for nothing,' growled Doug.

Hedy quickly told Bess about Albert Nobody's spirit at Hoarder Hill, and what she'd seen Cyrus do right before he had unleashed his sleep song on them. 'We have to stop him,' she said.

Bess used binoculars from his pack to survey the new bridge that had formed ahead of them. 'We need to get to that. It seems to run in towards what I hope is Northern Ireland, over the horizon.' He turned to them. 'Can you swim three kilometres?'

Hedy's mouth ran dry. She didn't answer, but seeing the looks on their faces, Bess said, 'I didn't think so.'

Gint huffed and puffed in the direction of the thunderhead cloud, making it roil upwards. As the haze lifted, the hexagonal columns of the Causeway began to shift. The straight road of stone pillars out towards the horizon became a huge loop that started at the bay, circled out for miles and then coiled back. It was not a still road, either. The columns themselves began to pump up and down like pistons through the sea's surface, churning the water. Cyrus and Gint were going to have to choose their footsteps carefully or else they'd find themselves falling into the sea.

Gront planted what looked like a massive, angled magnifying glass into the beach, then dusted his hands off. 'Ready yourselves,' he called.

Beatrice tugged Spencer backwards away from the shoreline as Gint and Cyrus lined up, but Spencer brushed her away impatiently.

'Steady yourselves!' yelled Gront.

Beatrice shook his arm more fiercely.

'What?' Spencer asked.

'I think,' she said, 'I think my grandfather is in Cyrus.'

Spencer froze. 'What? Are you sure?'

'I think I'm sure.'

*What did he do to Hedy?* Spencer thought, staring anxiously out to sea. 'Well, get him out! Do your exorcist thing!'

Beatrice hesitated, biting her lip.

'GO!' roared Gront.

They were off. Gint lunged forward and Cyrus leapt – higher and farther than Spencer had ever seen someone leap – away over the sea. The moment they hit the Causeway, Gront's oversized magnifying glass beamed the image of them up on to the clouds, like a live stream of the race.

'Hurry up!' Spencer urged Beatrice. She faced the Causeway and began muttering under her breath.

'What's all this about?' Stan said, butting his head in.

'Beatrice said Albert Nobody has taken over Cyrus!'

'No, not another one!' Stan gasped. 'Why does this always happen to us?'

They watched the cloud for a couple of moments, hoping for a sign that Nobody was being pulled from Cyrus, but instead Beatrice faltered and fell silent.

'Nothing's happening,' she said. 'I don't think I properly remembered the words that Rabble told me.'

'That was the only thing you had to remember!' Spencer cried.

'We can't let Nobody win,' said Max.

'Well, we can't let Gint win!' Stan added. 'That monstrous Gront will eat me in two bites! One of us will have to race and beat them both.'

'Do it, Spencer,' Max said.

'There's no way *I* can race them!'

'You can. What about the cheetah spots from the Mystify Me tent?'

Spencer had forgotten about the prize that he and the Woodspy had won. 'What if I'm still not fast enough?'

'Try,' Beatrice said, quietly but firmly. 'If you try, I'll try. If Cyrus gets back, I promise I'll try.'

They tore through Spencer's backpack, looking for the cheetah spots, and found that the curious Wood-spy had somehow opened the jar of slime. Now the goo was spread through the insides of the bag. Beatrice used the spurtle to scoop and wind up as much of the slime as she could, while Spencer and Max picked out the cheetah spots and peeled them from their backing paper.

'On the heels, on the heels,' Spencer said to himself nervously, whacking a black sticker on the backs of each of his trainers. At once an energy sizzled from his heels through his feet, zipped up his legs and then travelled right through the rest of him. It was a feeling of vitality, of corkscrewed momentum that was eager to spring free.

'I think they're for real!' he shouted, and then – to the hullabaloo of shocked giants yelling around the bay – he pelted down the rocky beach on to the pillars of the Giant's Causeway.

'My ginger boy is racing!' squealed the girl giant as his foot hit the first pillar.

It took a few strides for Spencer's eyes and mind to catch up with the speed of his legs. The hardest part was anticipating which rising and falling columns were going to be safely above the water for him to land on.

Hundreds of metres distant, Cyrus hurdled in massive bounds across the shifting pillars of the Causeway. A few paces behind him lumbered Gint, whose tread was so long and wide that losing a column here or there didn't make much difference to him. It seemed an impossible distance for Spencer to close ... except that the power rocketing from his feet felt endless, unstoppable, unbeatable.

A minute later, though, he made the wrong call and lost his footing when the column he was aiming for plunged below the water. He tumbled into the sea, gasping at the cold, and scrabbled for a handhold on a rising column to bring him back up. Soaked to the bone and spitting out a mouthful of salt water, he hauled himself to his feet and then kept on running. *It's just like hopscotch crossed with tag*, he thought to himself. A terrified part of him added, *where I could drown*.

Behind him, he heard distant chanting from the giants in their amphitheatre, words that sounded like, 'Roll them, bowl them! Roll them, bowl them!'

There was a rapid, rattling noise over his shoulder

and he turned around just in time to see objects like bowling balls speeding for him. *Whizzballs*, Spencer realized. At the very last moment, Spencer sprang, lifting his knees as high as he could, and the whizzballs shot underneath and along the Causeway, headed for Gint and Cyrus. *Hopscotch, tag* and *dodgeball*, he thought.

He risked a quick look up at the image in the cloud. It showed only Gint and Cyrus, which Spencer took to mean that he was so far from the lead that he wasn't worth showing. The whizzballs – only marbles to a giant – careered at Cyrus, one of them striking him in the leg. He pitched into the water with a splash, and Gint tromped past to take the lead, yelling something insolent. Cyrus's face twisted into a sneer that Spencer recognized immediately – it was most definitely an Albert Nobody expression. He made his way back on to the Causeway and ran for Gint's foot, managing to bring the giant to his hands and knees with a crash that shook the columns.

Their attacks on each other allowed Spencer to close the gap between them, the tortoise to their two battling hares. And once again, he re-characterized this race: *hopscotch, tag, dodgeball – and wrestling*. He wasn't sure what he'd do if he actually caught up with them.

Bess had no magical ability to transform Jelly's clog the way Cyrus had done.

'You should get a maker to make you an inflatable magic boat,' Jelly told him, 'for your next hunt.'

'Well, I realize that *now*,' said Bess testily.

'I'm kind of surprised you haven't thought of it before.'

'Can you bargain with whales?' Doug asked. 'Would a whale give us a ride?'

'Be serious,' scoffed Bess. 'Or at least be quiet, so I can think.'

'Well, we saw one earlier and we haven't exactly got a lot of options in the middle of the sea,' Doug pointed out.

Hedy closed her eyes, ignoring the squabble. It was impossible, however, to ignore the straining of the silvery ≈ mark in her hand and the rest of the map tattoos. They swam in her skin, in her face and neck, shoulder and arm, yearning to get closer to that sea bridge just over there; they would take her there, it would be so easy, all she had to do was walk towards it . . .

*Splash.*

In a trance, Hedy stepped off their tiny island into the swell of the sea, oblivious to the cries of the others. The magnetic pull of the map in her hand immediately began to drag her through the water, just as eagerly as in the slipstream. But Hedy was not a canoe, designed to float. She was heavy with clothes, shoes and backpack, as well as her own body weight, and she was metres below the water's surface. An indistinct form swam in the depths underneath her. Hedy didn't want to find out what it was. She kicked and flailed as hard as she could, trying to angle herself upwards.

Just when she thought her burning lungs would explode, her face broke the waterline. Hedy gulped at the air hungrily. But swimming whilst being dragged wasn't easy. And when she saw a long tentacle lash out of the water, not thirty metres away, she panicked. Seawater filled her mouth. Spluttering, she tried to turn her head enough to cough, but only sucked in more seawater.

That dreadful tentacle whipped up and through the air again. Was it closer this time? She twisted her head around and saw the distant forms of Jelly and Doug and Bess on the tiny island of pillars, yelling. With the map tattoos pulling her so strongly, there was no way she could fight her way back there. But the sea bridge was still so far away.

Five metres from her, the tentacle brushed up through the water's surface and Hedy let loose a scream. At that moment, a huge bubble shot up from below and exploded. The force of it flung Hedy and the tentacled creature away from each other. She gasped when she came up for air, terrified that the large shape rising up in front of her was that tentacled beast. But, to her shock, it was the rough crystal throne from the underground lake cavern, and sitting on it was the Kelpie King himself.

He leant down to offer a hand, which she grabbed readily, but he didn't haul her out of the water. Instead, he flashed his wily smile and said, '*It does not please the king to see you taken by the beast.*'

Hedy knew what he expected of her. Even though she was half-drowned, the rule-bound Kelpie King awaited a completion of the rhyme. She racked her brains, keeping a fretful eye on the water around her in case a tentacle made an appearance. What rhymed with *beast*? Finally, she managed to say, '*Thank you, I don't want to be the hungry monster's feast.*'

The Kelpie King nodded, satisfied, and lifted her from the water. Coughing at the base of his throne, Hedy looked in both directions. Now what? Jelly, Bess and Doug were back there, and the bridge was still at least two kilometres distant. She wondered whether she could turn the Kelpie King's ways to her advantage. On the pretext of regaining her breath, she thought and thought, and then finally asked,

*'Can you take my friends and I to the bridge that spans the sea?*

*'The magician's map is pulling me there. It's where I ought to be.'*

The king looked pleased, like a parent outfoxed by his child. *'You have rare nerve to make a throne the craft by which you flee.'*

## CHAPTER 27

## CHALLENGERS

Spencer was within a few hundred metres of Gint and Cyrus when out of the corner of his eye he spotted a strange object heading at speed towards the Causeway. Not quite boat-shaped, but – Spencer realized with a shiver – it seemed to be carrying people or creatures. He put his head down to run even faster, hoping to be far away when whatever it was landed.

Screeches overhead made him look up. It was Chit and Chat, flapping through the buffeting winds. The cockatoos wheeled out towards the thing that was travelling towards the bridge. *Be careful*, Spencer thought at them.

Ahead of him, Gint and Cyrus were making only sporadic headway. Cyrus had managed to catch one of the whizzballs and he hurled it at Gint – right between the legs. With an ear-splitting squeal of pain, Gint shrank like a deflating balloon, down to his original mere three or four metres. As the giant groaned over his injury, Cyrus began loping along the Causeway again.

'Stan's bear friend!' squawked Chit, swooping close by.

'What?' Spencer panted.

'Paw of Doom!' cawed Chat.

Spencer's heart leapt and he slowed to look back at the strange thing surging towards the Causeway. As it drew closer, he realized he could see Hedy, Jelly, Doug, Bess and a stranger with blue skin and a spiky crown upon his head. They were hanging on to . . . a small iceberg? No, it was a carved *throne*. Overcome with relief, Spencer stopped running.

Down the Causeway, Gint got to his hands and knees and barked something at the water, so loudly that even Cyrus looked over his shoulder to see what was happening. A moment later, a few metres off the bridge, the water convulsed. Without any other warning, two colossal tentacles struck out from the water and grabbed the escaping Cyrus around the shins. He screamed, clawing at the bridge, as the tentacles dragged him towards the edge. At last he managed to wrap his arms around one final pillar, and he held on for dear life, his legs still in the grip of the gigantic, bulbous squid that rose to the surface.

Cyrus awkwardly turned his head towards the water and tried to emulate the giant's low, booming bark. That only seemed to spur the creature on. It yanked at his legs – once, twice – and the third time Cyrus's hold came loose. He disappeared below the waves.

'Spence!' It was Hedy. She clambered up to the Causeway and dashed towards him. It was really her, here in the middle of the sea, hugging him so hard that the air squeezed out of his lungs.

At the very same time, they both burst out, 'Nobody has taken over Cyrus!' and then, 'How did *you* know?'

For a second, they allowed themselves a smile.

'Are you OK?' she asked.

Spencer nodded. 'You?'

'I think so.' She looked at him askance. 'Why are you jiggling?'

Pointing to the heel of his shoe, Spencer said, 'Cheetah spots. They make me want to run.'

They helped Jelly, Doug and Bess up on to the Causeway, but the strange blue man would not leave his throne.

'*You owe me a debt*,' he said to Hedy.

She nodded. '*I . . . I won't forget.*'

Satisfied, the king tapped his throne and it drew away from the Causeway, dropping into the sea.

There was no time to catch up because the water around the bridge was pulsing with resonating bursts. And then out of the water bounded Cyrus. The reaching tentacles in his wake didn't follow him, however; they twitched in Gint's direction, snaked around the half-giant and yanked him into the water with a tremendous spray.

Cyrus panted on the Causeway, staring smugly at Gint thrashing in the water. Then he glanced in their direction. 'Hello, Sang-spawn.' Without another word, he took off in his great soaring leaps.

'If Nobody wins the race, he gets the Loom piece,' said Spencer.

Hedy raised a hand, trembling with the shifting map tattoos. Of its own volition, her hand jerked out to sea where Gint flailed. 'But the map is ... we can't let that guy drown!'

'If we save him, I'll definitely never win the race!' Spencer exclaimed. 'And the rule is I have to beat him to win. I have to go now.'

'Spence,' said Jelly, 'you're my favourite ginger ninja in all the world, but you're not fast enough to beat Cyrus.'

Spencer drew himself as tall as he could. Maybe today was the day he could surprise everyone. 'Follow this bridge all the way. It leads to land where Max and Stan are. I'll see you there.'

Hedy nodded. 'See you there.'

'Show us how fast a cub like you can run,' said Doug with an affectionate nuzzle.

Spencer drew a deep breath and then unleashed the built-up power in his legs. He streaked away on Cyrus's tail, leaving Hedy and the others gaping.

'Help!' yelled the giant, interrupting them. His eyes were bulging as he fought to keep his head above water.

The tattoos wrenched in Hedy's skin again, pulling in the giant's direction. 'We have to save him.'

'With what?' said Bess. 'We're here for the Loom, Hedy, not to save the very creature keeping us from it.'

'The Kelpie King didn't have to save me, but he did!' said Hedy hotly.

'And what about the troll?' Jelly added. 'He didn't have to save us either, but he did!'

Reliving the stomach-dropping feeling of the Puzzlewood bridge slackening underneath her, Hedy suddenly thought of the troll's whisker. She ripped open her backpack and drew it out, but then stopped. 'It won't be long enough,' she said.

'Troll's whisker? It'll grow long enough,' said Bess.

With the columns pumping up and down, the only thing they could do to anchor their end of the whisker was to hold it. Hedy stood at the edge of the bridge and, like a cowboy, began whirling the end above her head.

'Hey!' she shouted at the giant. 'Grab hold!'

She cast the whisker out as hard as she could and it flicked out, reaching further and further, seeming to grow in that moment, until it slapped down right near the giant. He seized it. The four of them braced themselves with every ounce of strength, struggling to keep a steady foothold with the columns moving underneath. Hand over hand, the giant towed himself along, but he bellowed as his legs were yanked by the squid.

'I always hated tug-o'-war at school!' Jelly panted.

'We'll have to let go,' cried Bess as they struggled to haul the giant in. 'Or we'll end up in the water just like him!'

'We're not letting him drown,' Hedy insisted. She locked eyes with the giant and shouted, 'Come on!'

The giant choked out another cry, then held one of his hands to his lips and began to blow on his thumb until he was red in the face. He inflated at a terrific speed. His sudden bulk prised open the squid's painful grip, and the giant reached back and walloped the tentacle that held him. As it slithered into the water, the giant dragged himself the last ten or so metres to the Causeway and climbed up, towering over them. He barked at the squid in the water, like an owner of a disobedient dog, and then grunted at them, 'Thanks. Do you know who's winning?'

Cheetah spots or no cheetah spots, Spencer was starting to feel hot and sandpapery in the lungs. He'd never run so far or fast in his life, and he'd slowly managed to whittle down Cyrus's lead. How satisfying it had been to see Cyrus (*It's Nobody in there!* he kept reminding himself) looking over his shoulder anxiously. But now the shore was fast approaching. Was there enough distance for him to close the gap?

Suddenly, Cyrus turned and began bounding towards Spencer. Was he going to attack him, tackle him, like he had Gint? Instead, bizarrely, Cyrus began to sing. Spencer stumbled, utterly confused. And then he stopped entirely. Heavy drowsiness descended. If he'd just listen, a cocoon of rest awaited him, he could simply close his eyes and . . .

*Screech!* Through leaden eyelids, Spencer saw streaks of white and yellow swoop overhead, and then bursts of flame exploded all around Cyrus, cutting him off in mid-song. He immediately felt the drag of slumber evaporate.

'Help Spencer!' squawked Chit, dropping stones from his claws.

'Bombs away!' cried Chat, wheeling in the sky and releasing his own small missiles.

The cockatoos had Max's exploding grotesque pellets from the Foundry, and they were aiming them right at Cyrus.

Cyrus was too wet for his clothes to catch fire, but he yelped in pain as the pellets struck him. Spencer took his chance. He swerved around Cyrus and pelted along the Causeway, focusing for all he was worth on the end of the bridge, a kilometre away.

Not daring to check behind, Spencer forced his legs and arms to pump as fast as they could possibly go. Closer and closer the shore drew. The amphitheatre was hopping with excitable giants, all chanting something indecipherable. With half a kilometre to go, the shout resolved into a single word.

'Ginger! Ginger! Ginger!'

They were cheering *him*! Spurred on despite the sharp stitch in his side, he raced for the finish.

But in the corner of his eye was a flicker of movement. He risked a glance – Cyrus was catching up. He drew neck and neck, and then ahead. One hundred metres from the end of the Causeway, Cyrus twisted in mid-air and knocked into Spencer, who went sprawling.

Wincing in pain, Spencer looked up to see Cyrus already making his next leap ahead. He struggled to his feet and broke into a run again. But it was over. He'd never catch Cyrus now.

Except . . .

Storming down the Causeway was Stan. Sure-footed on the moving pillars, the stag closed the gap between him and Cyrus in seconds. He lowered his head and charged. Cyrus realized what was happening too late; he was jabbed with an antler as he tried to leap out of the way. It was shock, more than pain, that made him stagger.

*This* was Spencer's chance. He ignored his throbbing aches and sprinted for the end. There was Gront, holding a handkerchief the size of a tablecloth. Spencer put everything he had into a final burst of speed, and as he passed Gront, the cloth came fluttering down behind him, heavy as tarpaulin.

He'd won.

Max and Beatrice raced along the bay cheering, but their elation turned to fear as they spotted something behind him. He turned. Cyrus was stalking forward with a contemptuous look and his hands clenched like he was ready to strike. But before he could get within arm's reach, Beatrice planted herself in front of Spencer.

'Out of the way, Bea.' It was Nobody's sneering tone.

'No, Grandad,' said Beatrice gravely. 'You lost the race.'

'I beat the giant.' He looked up at Gront. 'That was the rule, wasn't it? Beat Gint?'

Gront murmured uncomfortably.

'That's what I've done,' he continued. 'So, when the little halfwit here unearths the third piece of the Loom, it'll join the two pieces I have already.'

'You mustn't use it!' cried Beatrice. 'It's too dangerous, you need to think this through.'

'You don't know what it's like,' he shot back. 'The threads tying my thoughts to my spirit – they're decaying, crumbling. I can't take this ghastly feeling of myself disintegrating any more. I need my own body. I need to unmake that choice to separate myself. I'm going back in time, back to before I fell ill. I'm weaving a different fate for myself and undoing that decision.'

'If you weave a different fate for yourself, aren't you changing everything for me and Dad too? What if Dad never meets Mum?'

'They're not together now, though, are they? It could save everyone a lot of trouble and upset.'

'But then . . . then I wouldn't be me,' Beatrice faltered.

'Perhaps it'll be for the better, Bea,' he said, wheedling. 'Perhaps you'll be a stronger magician then, one with ability so undeniable that you could win the Fantastikhana without me propping you up and tearing others down.'

'I might never be born at all.'

There was no answer from Beatrice's grandfather. The eyes that regarded her were as hard and pitiless as stone.

'By ... bone and blood ... I call you ...'

At his condescending look, Beatrice hesitated, panicking. The words Rabble had taught her seemed to have fled.

And then Chit screeched, 'By blood and bone, I call you out.'

'By blood and bone, I call you in,' answered Chat.

Beatrice straightened, resolute. 'By blood and bone, I call you out. By blood and bone, I call you in. By blood and bone, I call you down!'

At the final word, crackles of blue light rippled over Cyrus, and he fell to his hands and knees on the rocky shore. A hazy blue form slipped out of him – Albert Nobody.

The giants all around muttered fearfully.

Although he struggled and strained, Nobody's blue form flowed inexorably towards his trembling granddaughter. 'If you're going to call me down, you'll be fighting me for the rest of your life!' He abruptly ceased struggling against Beatrice's command and instead streaked towards her, as though to attack.

Max lunged forwards, jabbing the wooden spurtle with glittering slime on the end of it. 'Slime, get him!'

The Commandable Slime rocketed into the air, stretching like a net. Nobody's haze flew straight into it, and the slime closed around him, contracting into a blue blob and dropping to the ground.

'Slime, harden,' ordered Spencer.

They'd done it. They'd trapped Nobody.

When Hedy, Jelly, Doug and Bess made it to shore, carried by the galloping Gint, all thought of Verdandi's Loom fled for a few moments. It felt like months had passed since they had been together.

'Jelly, you're suffocating me!' Max laughed as his sister squeezed him.

'Enjoy it while it lasts,' she said, then she drew back, sharp-eyed. '*What* is going on with your hair?'

'Chit and Chat wanted to make a nest.'

The giants cheered excitedly when they thought Doug and Stan were racing towards each other to do battle but, to their disappointment, Doug reared up and clapped a paw on Stan's back. 'Give a rug a hug!' he exclaimed.

Stan sniffed his friend disapprovingly. 'You smell dreadful, Douglas. Like rotting crabs.'

'Travelling halfway around the world through land and sea will do that to anybody, Stan. True adventurers have to endure hardship, you know.'

'Adventurer? You're just lucky my poetic genius saved you from terminal hardship. What were you trapped by? Worms? Honestly, Doug, you should be ashamed of yourself.'

'You didn't see the size of those worms, you mousy twig-muncher!' Doug waved his white paw at his friend. 'For that you're going to have to carry me back. My paw is sore.'

'Are you out of your mind?' Stan exclaimed. 'You must be one and a half times my weight!'

As they argued – much to the amusement of the giants – Bess was having a quiet word with Cyrus. The young man looked heavy-hearted as he pulled the silvery frame and quartz ring of Verdandi's Loom from his pocket and handed them to the treasure hunter.

Gint knelt by Spencer and Hedy. 'You won the race.

The Loom piece is yours.'

'Where is it?' asked Spencer.

'The magician's map should know,' said Gint.

Hedy tugged up her sleeve. Over half of the tattoos had disappeared, and the ones that remained danced in her arm impatiently. At Gint's encouraging nod, she reached out and touched his boot – the one that had been a massive rock on the shore.

Just like at Puzzlewood and in the Kelpie King's underground cave, the black lines streamed through her fingers and spread in a branching web over the boot. The boot shattered and fell off Gint's foot.

''Scuse the smell,' Gint muttered as he lifted his toes.

All that was left was one bootlace, now a long strand of gold. The thread of Verdandi's Loom. Hedy picked it up, and the silvery ≈ mark in her hand vanished.

## CHAPTER 28

### SAMHAIN

Time flew as they walked from the Giant's Causeway back to the Fantastikhana. Except for Cyrus, everyone talked over everyone else to swap stories about what they'd seen and done. When they tramped out of the slipway into the cellar of Pick Pocket Parlour, the Parlour itself was empty of patrons.

'Where is everybody?' Bess asked the manager.

'Awards ceremony,' he answered. 'They went to see if Candice Harding has feathers growing out of her, 'cos rumour has it the Sleight were turned into birds!'

'If the awards ceremony is on, they must have been turned back,' Bess guessed.

'Yeah, according to the gossip, it was Rabble who fixed them. So I didn't bother going to the ceremony. All the good stuff covered up as usual.'

They followed the skirl of bagpipes from Pick Pocket Parlour to the main cavern, now crammed with people who'd come to watch the announcement of the tournament winners. All of the Sleight – Candice, Morten, Flora, even Ewan – were onstage, looking wholly human, although Candice now sported a brilliant peacock feather on her lapel. They couldn't see Grandpa John or Mrs Pal anywhere.

Spencer noticed Beatrice holding her breath as Candice named the top four competitors, but none of them turned out to be her. 'That's that, then, no mentor for me,' she murmured, resigned. 'Probably some juvenile magician's jail.'

'I doubt it. You caught a poltergeist and saved the Fantastikhana, didn't you?' said Spencer.

'I was saving *myself*.'

'Just don't tell them that bit. Maybe Rabble will still tutor you. Best Slip engineer around, right?'

Beatrice's look told him it was a poor consolation.

As Candice declared the competition over, Doug and Stan suddenly gasped in dismay. Both were sinking to the ground rapidly; Doug's legs and body were flattening, and Stan's were fading away altogether.

'Oh no, the Whisker Wish is wearing off,' said Beatrice. 'It was competition magic, and the competition's over.'

'Can you recreate it?' asked Stan worriedly.

Beatrice looked crestfallen. 'I don't know if I can. I think my grandfather helped me.'

'Well, we're not freeing him just so we can gad about on four legs,' said Doug.

'You're right, Douglas,' Stan sighed. 'So, who's going to carry us?'

They found Grandpa John and Mrs Pal waiting for them in the Peacock Chamber.

'Bogs saved the day!' screeched Chit and Chat as Hedy and Spencer threw themselves at Grandpa John.

He hugged them tightly, and folded Jelly and Max in as well. 'Are you all right? Is anyone hurt?'

'We're fine,' said Hedy, and then all of them began talking at once to fill in Grandpa John and Mrs Pal.

Cyrus lingered in the doorway, downcast, until Flora drew him inside and began fussing over the cut on his chin. Candice strode to their side with a white cloth napkin and a glass of water to clean the wound. 'What were you *thinking*?' she demanded.

With a nod towards the huddle around Grandpa John, Cyrus said, 'I was thinking I don't have family like that.'

Candice looked hurt. She tossed the cloth and banged the glass down on the table, then awkwardly put her arms around him. 'Oh, you silly boy. Do you think the only reason I sent Bess after you was to get the Loom? You falling off a bridge, or drowning, or getting crushed by giants is not my idea of bringing you home safely, you know. How can we bring you up if we can't bring you home?'

Hedy could see Cyrus trying to resist what was clear: the love that Candice and the Sleight felt for him, although they may not have ever used the word. But finally, Cyrus buried his face in Candice's shoulder. Perhaps, thought Hedy, it was the first time in a long time.

After a while, Morten asked everyone to gather around the table. 'Enough of everybody having only some of the truth. We need to hear things from start to finish.'

And so, with the blob of hardened slime placed safely in a cast-iron box with Albert Nobody trapped inside, the children and Bess told them everything, from Puzzlewood and the Kelpie King to the race at the Giant's Causeway. Beatrice stoically endured the Sleight's stern questioning over her part in bringing Nobody to the Fantastikhana. Against Spencer's advice, she also admitted that she had stopped her grandfather because she'd been afraid of being woven out of existence; she hadn't known at the time that she was also saving the Fantastikhana.

'But she did put things right in the end,' said Spencer.

'And I will vouch that she did so with courage,' Stan added.

Candice shared a look with the rest of the Sleight before she spoke. 'Agreed. However, we have to formally disqualify you from the tournament, Beatrice.'

Beatrice flushed. 'I know. We saw the winners being announced. Even with Grandad trying to cheat for me, I'm not good enough.' She pointed at the iron casket. 'What are you going to do with my grandfather?'

'We won't rush a decision,' said Candice. 'Ewan will take you to your father now. We'll call you both in tomorrow to talk it over, before you go back over-ground.'

Beatrice got to her feet, mumbled goodbye and headed towards the door.

'Oh, and Beatrice,' Candice called out. 'Don't let this hold you back. Perhaps with the right mentor, we'll see you back here on your own merits in a couple of years.'

With Beatrice gone and the cast-iron box removed, the Sleight and their guests went back to the most important matter at hand: Verdandi's Loom. Bess carefully arranged the silver frame (which had grown even bigger), the dark and clear quartz ring, and the golden thread at the centre of the table. Each piece was beautiful on its own, but Hedy sensed that the whole Peacock Chamber was imagining what the Loom would look like, what it would feel like, when it took its true form. Even Grandpa John, the most resistant of anyone there, couldn't mask a certain hunger in his eyes.

'I tracked down a very old diary account that

explains how it works,' said Flora. 'There's a specific incantation, and the stone must hang from the frame by the thread, like a pendulum. If the thread is connected to the darker half of the ring, that takes you back to the past. If the thread is holding the clear half of the ring – that's for the future. But if you loop the thread right on the join where the dark quartz meets the clear – where the past meets the future – that will pause the present.'

'What are you going to do with it?' Hedy asked softly. Having gone through so much to get the Loom, she felt a protective sense of kinship for it. 'How will you keep it safe?'

'Only pausing time has any chance of passing un-detected by the others' monitoring,' said Candice. 'The danger of someone trying to use it to weave the past or future and breaking the Pact is too great. Any one of us might be weak enough to want to turn back time at some point.' She sighed. 'We need to separate them again, and this time do a better job of keeping them apart.'

'How far apart is far enough,' asked Mrs Pal, 'when the distance between continents can be shrunk so easily by the Slip?'

The bleak silence of the Sleight spoke volumes.

'What if,' said Hedy, her eyes on the forlorn Cyrus, 'what if a piece was hidden in another dimension? One that no one here can get to, except for a split second, every ten years?' Cyrus looked up and sat on the edge of his chair. 'Would that be far enough?'

Edinburgh was quiet. It was nearing midnight, and the public gardens below the castle were closed. But that didn't stop their group slipping into the gardens, via a reversed staircase leading upwards from the vaults, much like the one they had descended near the Palisade.

'I have to be able to deny use of the Loom,' Candice had told Grandpa John as she had handed him the pieces of Verdandi's Loom. 'So I'd like you to chaperone Cyrus to the cusp between this world and the Aos Sí lands.'

'Aren't you worried I'll use it to go back in time, become the greatest magician alive?' Grandpa John had asked.

'No,' Candice had smiled. 'You're as paranoid as we are. You're one of us.' And then she had returned to the private, quiet dinner that Cyrus was having with the Sleight.

Now, overground, the children and Grandpa John waited with Cyrus beside the great iron fountain of cherubs, mermaids and animal heads. Nearby in one of the hotel's luggage wagons, Doug and Stan were packed, bickering about who was squashing whom.

'You know,' Cyrus said to the bear and the stag, 'if you come with me, I bet the Aos Sí could restore you to your full bodies. It'd be just like these past couple of days. You could go wherever you want.'

Doug and Stan gaped at him, considering the offer.

'It's tempting, cub,' said Doug with a sidelong glance at Stan. 'But . . .'

'But *these* are our people. Our tribe,' finished Stan. 'We belong with them.'

'And look at us. Bodiless though we are, we're out and about in our nifty little cart,' Doug pointed out.

At a few minutes to midnight, a breeze rustled the trees of the gardens.

'You'll need to be ready when the cusp is here,' Grandpa John said to Cyrus. He shook the teenager's hand. 'I wish you luck, Cyrus. I hope your mother's people welcome you back as you deserve.'

'Thank you, Mr Sang.'

Cyrus said his goodbyes to the boys, and then Jelly

flung her arms around his neck, sniffing. 'Look after yourself,' she said. 'Don't forget me.'

'How could I?' he said, kissing her on the cheek. And finally he turned to Hedy. 'Thanks, Hedy. For convincing Candice this was a good idea.'

There was a stubborn lump in Hedy's throat. She gave him a hard hug, not knowing what to say.

Before the right words came to her, the fountain's iron women and cherubs shifted, their robes rustling as they murmured, '*Samhain, Samhain.*'

'I've made sure the thread is right on the join between the past and future halves of the stone,' Grandpa John reminded Cyrus. 'When you're over the cusp, leave the thread and the stone on this side. I'll hide one, and the Sleight will take care of the other. The frame of the Loom goes with you.'

A heavy mist was rising between the trees. 'Is that where the cusp will be?' Cyrus asked, his voice shaky.

Grandpa John handed Verdandi's Loom to Cyrus and laid a comforting hand on his shoulder. 'The way home lies before you. Take it.'

Haltingly at first, Cyrus began walking towards the mist in the trees. He stopped before becoming lost from view, and stuck the silver frame in the grass, ready to swing the stone ring on its golden thread.

'Cyrus,' Hedy hurried to his side and grasped his arm, 'maybe we'll see you in ten years.'

'Hope so,' Cyrus smiled. 'You're good at that stuff.'

And then she was holding thin air. Cyrus had vanished. The women and angels of the iron fountain were perfectly still, the mist was gone. It was a normal midnight in Edinburgh. And in Hedy's jacket pocket were the thread and stone of Verdandi's Loom.

## CHAPTER 29

## AFTER ALL

The next morning, the Chinese stone lion in the garden at Hoarder Hill roared for the first time in many years. It split straight down the middle, as though being unzipped, opening down to a tunnel in the earth. Out of the tunnel came the children and Grandpa John, and also Ewan and his cockatoos.

They had walked Mrs Pal to her staircase near the Palisade, where Soumitra was eagerly waiting. And then, promising to return soon for Grandpa John's car, they had continued walking, thanks to a new slipway created by Brock Rabble.

'John, are you sure you don't mind this slipway being made permanent?' said Ewan, peering curiously around the garden.

'As long as Bucephalus puts someone trustworthy on to guard it,' Grandpa John said. 'I don't want all and sundry to come knocking.'

'I'll have a word with Mr Boo,' Ewan assured him. He hesitated and looked around at them all. 'I guess this is goodbye, then.'

Grandpa John frowned. 'Don't you want to meet the rest of your family?'

The back door of the house flew open and Grandma Rose, Mum and Dad – returned from his charity bike ride – hurried down the garden path to meet them.

Ewan beamed. 'Aye, I'd love that.'

They picnicked on the back lawn for much of the day, enjoying the autumn sunshine after days underground.

'I want to hear absolutely everything,' Grandma Rose said, feeding Chit and Chat some apple from her hand.

So Hedy, Spencer, Jelly and Max recounted their adventures from the first moment they met Ewan to

Cyrus's return home. Doug insisted on Spencer wearing him like a cape to help Hedy and Jelly re-enact the bridge jumps in Puzzlewood. And when they came to the challenge of the Kelpie King, Stan had them all in stitches with his mouth and throat warm-up exercises, like a singer getting ready for a big performance.

Later, climbing the sycamore that presided over the hill, Max said, 'I wish we could build a treehouse in this tree like Beatrice's blanket fort. One that was super massive on the inside.'

'Yes!' Spencer whooped. 'With . . . with a control room to raise the ladder. And an ice creamery.'

'And a parkour room.'

'Indoor waterslides!' Spencer's mind bounced between all these possibilities, wondering whether Beatrice would have been able to create them. 'Grandpa John,' he said, 'I think you should be Beatrice's mentor.'

Grandpa John grunted, dubious. 'She wouldn't want an out-of-practice old grump like me.'

'You never know, John,' said Ewan with a wink. 'I think the Sleight might like that idea.'

Jelly tugged Hedy by the arm, and they wandered down the garden. 'Look what I found hidden in my back pocket,' Jelly said, pulling something from her jeans. It was one of the fortunes Maureen had typed for Cyrus. On the back was a rather good drawing of the girls, Doug and Cyrus in a canoe, and he'd written on it, *Don't forget me either*. 'I wonder how he's getting on,' Jelly said. 'I wonder if his abilities have come back like he was hoping.'

Hedy gave her arm a squeeze. 'Who needs abilities, right? We did OK for a couple of giftless bogs.' She glanced at Max. 'Maybe we can pass off his moustache as a gift.'

'I don't know whether I'm glad or sad that Mrs Pal found some counter-ointment for him. Convincing him to use it will be the hard part. Might have to slather him when he's sleeping.'

Hedy threw her head back and laughed, her hood dropping off on to her shoulders. Jelly joined in, glanced at Hedy, and gasped.

'What is it?' Hedy asked.

With a delicate touch just behind Hedy's ear, Jelly said, 'There's a tiny black mark, right here. It's kind of squiggling.'

Hedy's heart jumped. 'Is it the map?'

'I think so.'

*A living map*, thought Hedy, *a magician's map.* After one anxious heartbeat, an image of Bess unexpectedly popped into her mind. She began to wonder . . . could the map be grown? Could it be moored to new instructions, set to find other hidden treasures of the past? Grinning, Hedy pulled her cousin back towards their family at the crest of the hill, feeling that she had been gifted something remarkable after all.

## ACKNOWLEDGEMENTS

Much of *The Magician's Map* was written as the tragedy of the pandemic spread across the world. Although we were not able to see many of our friends and loved ones in person, they had our backs from afar. Naming everyone in our cheer squad would make the 'Acknowledgements' as long as the book itself so we have to rein it in, but your support for the first book was the jet fuel we needed to write this one – thank you.

We particularly want to shine a light on:

The Holland family & Heidi Gomes for their continued support and encouragement, Lia Brandligt, Heather Pretty, Dijanna Mulhearn, Dede Grutz, Susie Steadman, Tina Stripp, Kat Rallis, Josef & Susan

Mucha, Naomi Watts, Elizabeth Berkley, Keira Newton (for our first ever school visit!), Bob Goodman, Dan Baldwin, Damien and Bjorn Puckler, Agrita, Lexi, Nick and Ophelia de Toth, Sophie & Kate, Mary Liz and the Shack Artists team, Jaimie and Chris Kollmer, the wonderful squad at Tales by Mail, and all the fabulous crew at Better Read Than Dead bookstore.

For bringing *The House on Hoarder Hill* to life with their chapter readings (check out YouTube!) we thank Jenny Richardson, Cain Fowler and Paddy Holland (aka our Spencer).

We extend Gint-sized high-fives to our fabulous test readers for their thoughtful feedback and letting us know we were on the right track: Matilda Brooks, Connor Chung, Sylvie De Toth, Jamie Olds, Adrian Yeung and Charlotte Yeung.

And to all the kids around the world (including grown-up kids!) whom we do not know but who embraced *The House on Hoarder Hill*, we thank you from the bottom of our hearts and owe you trolls' whiskers (sorry, our supply chain is currently disrupted).

We couldn't have done it without our amazing literary agents, Oliver and Paula Latsch at LatschLit.

Their no-holds-barred advice (whether we like it or not!), friendship and humour are priceless in helping us push forward and navigate new territory.

Special thanks to Rachel Leyshon, our ever-perceptive editor and Snowy Paw of Doom, who once again helped us find the story that needed to shine through, and to Laura Myers and Helen Jennings for making the story as clear and watertight as can be.

Heartfelt thanks to the whole Chicken House team – Barry Cunningham, Elinor Bagenal, Rachel Hickman, Jazz Bartlett Love, Sarah Wallis-Newman – who turned our ideas into actual books in actual bookstores around the world.

We're in awe of Maxine Lee-Mackie yet again for her cover artwork – so beautiful, mysterious, spooky and inviting all at once.

Huge thanks to Helen Masterton at Scholastic Australia and Samantha Palazzi at Scholastic USA for putting up with all our questions and flying the flag in our respective home territories. Thanks also to Catrin Abert at Piper Verlag for her continuing faith in Hedy and Spencer!

We remain so very grateful to our TV development team: Olivia Blaustein, Jamie Stockton and Maria

Snyder at CAA, Sam Raimi, Debbie Liebling, Zainab Azizi and Zach Berman at Pod 3, Nne Ebong, Hope Hartman, Casey Larson and Amy Ma at wiip.

From Kelly:

My love and thanks to:

Jeanette Wu, Josephine Wu, Richard Yip and Alex Yip for their care in so many ways, from the roof over my head and sweet treats to emergency medical advice.

The 'Chais', Doug (the Rug) Ngai and Kristen Cherrie, for their tireless PR and supportive skulduggery.

My folks, Juliana and Michael Ngai, who always encourage me with their pride, curiosity, cooked meals, washed laundry and too much else to list.

Brent Armfield, for pumping up my tyres, making life fun and knowing me so well.

And Rufus and Xavier, for being full of dreams and a source of wonder to me every day.

From Mikki:

Chris, Jen, Emily and Amy Taday for your friendship and love and giving me a roof above my head and a bed for my various flights to London. Charlie Brokenshire for unknowingly being my inspiration for kids that love magic! And I still will forever more need to always thank Doug Ngai for introducing me to his sister!

Mikki's family: Uldis, Martins, Amanda, Gint (the Giant), Sharon, Adrian, Thorley, Aleks, Josie, Annika, Ryan Silins and Bella Lish for their continued love and encouragement and unsolicited advice!

Colin Lish for being my rock and being the most amazing gift in my life. I love you.

In loving memory of: Ilze Ludmilla Vita Silins (aka Mrs Vilums), Sandra Waizer, Aina Lide, Jana Hale and Tom Grutz (Cora and Carsten's 'Papa').